Helix Shadows

Paul D. Zartman

Helix Shadows

Dedication

This is dedicated to my wife and kids, the people who never gave up on me and told me I could do anything I set my mind to. My kids helped inspire this book; you can even find their names in it. Thank you for never giving up on me and believing in me no matter what!

Chapter 1: The Signal

The afternoon sunbathed Shadowridge in a golden hue, its rays glinting off the rusting metal of the town's abandoned factory and casting long shadows over Main Street. In the heart of Ohio, Shadowridge seemed like any other small town. The streets were lined with faded storefronts, a mom-and-pop diner, and a record store with its iconic neon sign buzzing faintly. But beneath the seemingly idyllic surface lay an undercurrent of unease, whispered rumors of strange occurrences, and a tension the locals rarely spoke about out loud.

In Sarah's basement, the heart of the friend group's hangouts, the buzz of activity was anything but ordinary. Stacks of video game cartridges cluttered the coffee table, and a half-finished game of *Mortal Kombat* paused on the TV screen. Jamari, or Jam, as everyone called him, adjusted his thick glasses and tinkered with a cassette recorder.

Jamari, the group's tech wizard, had always been the one to fiddle with gadgets and unearth strange signals. As a kid, he'd spent hours dismantling his parents' old VCR to figure out how it worked. His fascination with technology had made him an outcast at school—until Alex befriended him in fifth grade, punching a bully who'd tried to steal Jam's calculator.

"I swear this thing's picking up some weird interference," Jam muttered, holding the recorder closer to his ear. The static crackled faintly, interspersed with a rhythmic beeping sound. "It's not a station, that's for sure."

"Maybe it's aliens!" Max said, his voice dripping with mock seriousness as he leaned back against the beanbag chair. He wore his usual colorful, mismatched socks, one with a Tamagotchi clipped. "Or maybe your cassette recorder is just as busted as your dial-up modem."

Max was the group's joker, always quick with a quip or a pun. Growing up in a household of five siblings, humor became his armor and weapon. During a summer at Shadowridge's roller rink, he'd met Sarah, who'd been trying—and failing—to balance on skates. His jokes had broken the ice, and Sarah soon introduced him to Alex and Jam.

"Shut up, Max," Jam retorted, his ears reddening. "I'm telling you, it's something."

"Something boring," Max quipped. "Sarah, back me up here."

Sarah, the group's voice of reason, glanced up from the *Lisa Frank* notebook she'd been doodling in. Sarah came from the wealthiest family in Shadowridge, but she'd never fit in with the other rich kids. They'd mocked her love for video games and comics, calling her a "wannabe nerd." Her friendship with Alex was forged during a school library campaign to allow comic books to be stocked.

"If Jam thinks it's important, maybe it is," she said diplomatically. "But it's probably just..."

A sudden tremor rattled the basement. The TV flickered, the image of the paused game distorting into a swirl of static before blinking off completely. The lights followed, plunging the room into darkness.

"What the...?" Alex's voice cut through the silence. As the group's unspoken leader, his instinct was to stand, flashlight in hand. "Is everyone okay?"

Alex's role as the leader stemmed from his unshakable sense of loyalty. Growing up with a single mom who worked long hours, he'd learned to take charge early. His first act of leadership had been defending Jam, but his quiet determination kept the group together through middle school drama and high school pressures.

"Not cool," Logan muttered from the corner, his combat boots scuffing the floor as he stood. Logan was the newest addition to the group, having moved to Shadowridge just a few months ago. His edgy style and aloof demeanor had initially kept the others at bay, but Alex had reached out after noticing Logan sitting alone at lunch.

"What just happened?" Logan asked.

Before anyone could answer, a loud boom echoed through the town, shaking the ground and sending objects tumbling from the shelves. They rushed to the small, high-set window, struggling to see through the gloom. A faint orange glow rose in the distance, accompanied by a plume of black smoke curling into the sky.

"That's the old Helix Labs site," Sarah said, trembling. "Something's happening there."

Jamari grabbed his pager and frantically punched in a few buttons. "We need to check this out. I mean, this is Helix Labs we're talking about. That place has been sealed off for years."

Alex hesitated. "It could be dangerous. We don't even know what's going on."

"Or it could be awesome," Max said, slipping on his sneakers. "Come on, Alex. When have we ever just sat back and done nothing?"

"He's right," Sarah added. "We need to see at least what's going on."

Logan crossed his arms. "You're all crazy. You know that, right?"

Alex exhaled sharply, his gaze flicking between the faint glow in the distance and his friends. "Fine. But we're sticking together. Everyone grabs a flashlight and a jacket. Let's go."

The ride through Shadowridge on their bikes was eerily quiet. The steady hum of unease drowned out the usual sounds of crickets and distant dogs barking. They pedaled quickly, the orange glow growing brighter as they approached the edge of town.

The Helix Labs site loomed ahead, a stark silhouette against the fiery backdrop. Once a hub of scientific innovation, the facility had been abandoned after a mysterious incident years ago. Now, it was nothing but crumbling walls and shattered windows, or so they'd thought.

"Whoa," Max whispered, skidding to a halt. "This... this looks like something out of a movie."

Flames licked the sky, illuminating the building's twisted metal and rubble. The air smelled of burnt chemicals, sharp and acrid. As they drew closer, Alex held up a hand, signaling the group to stop.

"Look," he said, pointing toward a cluster of figures near the wreckage. Men in hazmat suits moved methodically through the debris, some carrying strange, glowing equipment. Black vans were parked nearby, their headlights cutting through the smoke.

"Government?" Logan guessed.

"Has to be," Jam said, his voice low. "But what are they doing?"

"We need to get closer," Alex said.

Sarah grabbed his arm. "Are you crazy? They'll see us."

"Not if we're careful," Alex replied, his tone firm. "We need to figure out what's going on here. Jam, you've got that cassette recorder, right? Let's see if we can pick up anything they're saying."

Jamari nodded, pulling the cassette recorder from his backpack. They crept closer, keeping low behind a ridge of dirt and rubble. The voices of the men in hazmat suits carried faintly on the wind.

"...containment breach... subject is still unaccounted for..."

"Prepare for secondary extraction..."

"What subject?" Max whispered. "What are they talking about?"

Before anyone could answer, a sharp, inhuman screech pierced the air, sending shivers down their spines. The men froze, their heads snapping toward the sound. The group ducked lower, their hearts pounding in unison. They pressed themselves flat against the dirt mound, eyes wide as the scene unfolded.

The source of the screech remained hidden, but the tension among the hazmat-suited figures was palpable. One of them barked into a handheld radio, their words sharp and clipped.

"Initiate containment procedures. Deploy Unit 5 immediately!"

The ground trembled again, with a metallic groan echoing from the wreckage. Jam clutched the walkie-talkie tightly, and the static morphed into a cacophony of beeps and distorted voices.

"Did you hear that?" he whispered. "It's... it's not just interference anymore."

Max's face paled, his usual grin nowhere to be found. "What is it, Jam? What's happening?"

"I don't know," Jam admitted, his voice trembling. "But it's big."

"We should leave," Sarah said urgently, her voice a hushed plea. "Whatever this is, it's way over our heads."

Before Alex could respond, a massive shadow shifted within the wreckage. A figure emerged, hunched and otherworldly, its glowing eyes cutting through the smoke like twin beacons. The group's breath hitched simultaneously. The creature—if it could even be called that—moved with an unnatural grace, its limbs elongated and sharp. It paused, head tilting as if listening.

One of the hazmat-suited figures raised a device resembling a high-tech rifle and aimed it at the creature. "Engage on my mark," the figure commanded, their voice amplified by a speaker. "Steady... steady..."

The creature's head snapped toward the group's hiding spot. For a heart-stopping moment, glowing eyes locked onto Alex's. Time seemed to freeze as an icy chill coursed through him. Then, the creature let out a guttural roar that reverberated through the air, shaking the ground beneath them.

"Run!" Alex shouted, scrambling to his feet. The others didn't need to be told twice. They bolted back toward their bikes, chaos erupting behind them. The crack of energy weapons, the roar of the creature, and the shouts of the hazmat team blended into a cacophony of terror.

Logan was the first to reach his bike, his combat boots skidding on the dirt. "Move it!" he yelled, glancing back to see Sarah struggling with her flashlight, which had slipped from her jacket pocket.

"Leave it!" Alex urged, grabbing her arm and pulling her forward.

They pedaled as fast as their legs would allow, the fiery glow of Helix Labs shrinking behind them. But the feeling of those glowing eyes bore into Alex's mind, an unshakable dread that whispered: this wasn't over.

The group burst into Sarah's basement, slamming the door shut behind them. Their breaths came in ragged gasps, their faces pale and slick with sweat. The usual clutter of video games and comics felt eerily out of place after the chaos they'd just fled.

"What... what was that thing?" Max panted, collapsing onto the beanbag chair. His mismatched socks were caked with dirt, and his Tamagotchi dangled precariously from his ankle.

"I don't know," Alex admitted, pacing the room. His flashlight was still clutched tightly in his hand, the knuckles white. "But it saw us. I... I know it saw us."

"And those government guys?" Logan added, leaning against the wall. His arms were crossed, but his shaky voice betrayed his calm demeanor. "They had weapons... high-tech ones. What kind of stuff are they messing with out there?"

Jamari sat cross-legged on the floor, rewinding the cassette recorder. The static-filled sounds played back, crackling with distorted voices and faint screeches. "This isn't normal," he said, his voice low. "Helix Labs was supposed to be abandoned. Whatever's happening there now... it's big. Way bigger than we thought."

Sarah dropped onto the couch, her face pale. She pulled her legs up, wrapping her arms around her knees. "It's not just that thing," she said softly. "There was something about the way those men acted. Like they were... hunting it."

"Hunting it?" Max repeated, sitting up. "Okay, cool, so we've got monsters and monster hunters. Shadowridge just turned into a bad episode of *The X-Files*."

Alex shot him a glare. "This isn't funny, Max."

"I'm not trying to be funny," Max snapped back. "I'm trying not to freak out! What if that thing..." He trailed off, his usual bravado faltering. "What if it's still out there? Looking for us?"

"It is," Logan said grimly. All eyes turned to him. "Think about it. It looked right at us. It knows what we look like. It's not just going to let us go."

"But why us?" Sarah asked, her voice trembling. "We didn't do anything. We were just... in the wrong place at the wrong time."

Jamari tapped the recorder thoughtfully. "Maybe. Or maybe we saw something we weren't supposed to. Those guys in hazmat suits? They didn't look too happy about us being there."

"So what do we do now?" Max asked, his voice tinged with desperation. "Call the cops? Tell them we saw some government conspiracy stuff?"

"And say what?" Alex countered. "That we saw a monster and a bunch of secret agents? They'd think we're crazy."

"Maybe we should lay low," Sarah suggested. "Stay away from Helix Labs, from anything weird. Just pretend none of this happened."

Logan shook his head. "You think that thing will let us forget about it? If it wanted to, it could've..." He paused, swallowing hard. "It could've done much worse than just staring at us."

"He's right," Jamari said reluctantly. "We can't ignore this. Whatever's going on at Helix Labs... it's not just going to go away."

Alex stopped pacing, his jaw set. He looked around at his friends, their faces etched with fear and uncertainty. "We stick together," he said firmly. "No matter what happens, we're a team. We'll figure this out. But for now, we stay quiet and try to figure out what we're dealing with."

Sarah nodded hesitantly. Max muttered something about needing a break from "paranormal nonsense" but didn't argue further. Logan crossed his arms, his expression unreadable.

"So, what's step one of 'figuring it out'?" Max asked after a moment.

Alex glanced at Jamari. "What did you get on the tape?"

Jamari rewound it, adjusting the volume. The static-filled playback filled the room, broken by faint voices.

"...containment breach... subject is still unaccounted for..."

The group listened in silence, each word raising more questions than answers.

"Subject?" Sarah repeated. "What does that mean?"

"It means whatever that thing is," Logan said, his voice low, "the government knows about it. And they've been keeping it locked up."

"Until now," Alex added grimly.

The room fell into an uneasy silence. Outside, the faint sounds of crickets and distant traffic seemed almost mocking in their normalcy. Whatever had been unleashed at Helix Labs was out there, and the group couldn't shake the feeling that their lives had just been irreversibly changed.

The alarm clock buzzed insistently, jolting Alex awake. He groaned, smacking the off button before rolling out of bed. Monday mornings were never his favorite, but facing a typical school day felt almost surreal after the weekend events.

The streets of Shadowridge were quieter than usual as Alex pedaled his bike to school, his mind replaying the terrifying events at Helix Labs. He spotted Jamari waiting at the corner. Jam's bulky backpack sagged with his usual gear, but his face bore an uncharacteristic look of worry.

"Morning," Jam muttered, falling into step beside Alex. "You think... they'll say something about what happened?"

"No idea," Alex replied. "But they have to. Half the town probably saw that explosion."

As they arrived at school, the unusual sight of black government vans parked in front of the main building made Alex's stomach churn. A group of serious-looking men and women in dark suits stood near the entrance, their eyes scanning the students filing in. He spotted Logan leaning against the bike rack; his arms crossed as he glared at the agents.

"Well, this is new," Logan said as Alex and Jam approached. "You think they're here to brainwash us into forgetting what we saw?"

"If they were, they'd probably start with you," Max said, appearing behind them with his usual grin, though it didn't quite reach his eyes. "You're the most paranoid out of all of us."

Sarah arrived last, clutching a Lisa Frank folder tightly to her chest. She looks nervously at the agents before hurrying to the group. "This can't be good," she murmured.

The bell rang, and the students were herded into the gymnasium instead of their usual homerooms. The entire school buzzed with whispers as Principal Reynolds took the microphone. Tension overshadowed his typically genial demeanor as he gestured to the suited figures standing behind him.

"Good morning, everyone," Principal Reynolds began, his voice faltering slightly. "As many of you may have noticed, there was an incident this weekend at the old Helix Labs site. These representatives from the Federal Safety Administration are here to provide some information and answer your questions."

One of the agents, a tall man with graying hair and a piercing gaze, stepped forward. "Good morning, students. My name is Agent Rourke. I'm here to assure you that the situation at Helix Labs is under control. There is no danger to the public. The explosion resulted from a minor industrial accident during a routine clean-up operation."

Alex felt a ripple of unease. "Minor accident" hardly described what they'd seen.

"Why were there hazmat suits and vans?" a voice called from the bleachers. Alex turned to see Logan smirking, his hand still raised after asking the question.

Rourke's expression didn't change. "Safety precautions," he replied smoothly. "When dealing with older facilities, it's standard procedure. There's nothing to be concerned about."

Max leaned over to Alex. "That guy could be an alien in disguise, and I'd believe it."

"Shh," Sarah hissed. "They'll hear you."

The assembly continued, with Rourke fielding questions from curious and skeptical students alike. The more he spoke, Alex felt confident that the agent's words were carefully chosen to obscure the truth. When the bell finally rang, the group regrouped in the hallway.

"That was... a whole lot of nothing," Logan said, slamming his locker shut. "They didn't answer anything real."

"What did you expect?" Jam replied. "If they admitted what we saw, this place would be swarming with reporters."

Alex nodded. "We need to keep our heads down for now. They're watching everyone. If they figure out we were there…"

"We're screwed," Max finished. "Cool. Guess we're living in a spy movie now."

Sarah hesitated, glancing over her shoulder at the agents lingering by the office. "What if they already know?" she whispered. "What if they're waiting for us to slip up?"

Alex placed a hand on her shoulder. "We stick to the plan," he said firmly. "Act normal. Please don't talk about it where anyone can hear. We'll figure this out, but we have to be smart."

The group nodded in agreement, but tension lingered as they filed into their following classes. Despite the agent's reassurances, the feeling of being watched never left them.

The final bell rang, signaling the end of the school day. Alex slung his backpack over his shoulder, letting out a sigh of relief. The tension from the morning's assembly had followed him through every class, and he wasn't the only one. As they filed out of the building, he noticed the agents' black vans still parked out front, a subtle reminder that their lives were far from normal.

"Pizza?" Max asked, sliding up next to him with a hopeful grin. "Because I could seriously use a distraction that involves greasy food and terrible arcade games."

Alex nodded. "Yeah. Let's get everyone."

The group gathered near the bike racks, Logan already leaning against his with his usual air of nonchalance. "So, are we pretending everything's fine, or will we discuss this mess?"

"Both," Sarah said quickly, adjusting the strap of her bag. "But first, pizza."

The Shadowridge Pizza Palace wasn't fancy but a beloved hangout spot for kids and families alike. The neon sign above the entrance flickered, casting a colorful glow onto the sidewalk. Inside, the smell of melted cheese and pepperoni mixed with the beeping and buzzing of old arcade machines.

"Large pepperoni, extra cheese," Sarah said as she approached the counter, speaking like she'd rehearsed it a hundred times. She handed over a crumpled bill while Max and Jam made a beeline for the arcade corner.

"I've got next on Mortal Kombat," Max declared, digging quarters out of his pocket. "Jam, prepare to lose."

"In your dreams," Jam replied, already selecting his favorite character.

Logan lingered by the jukebox, flipping through the song selections with a faint look of amusement. Meanwhile, Alex and Sarah slid into a booth near the window, the warm light of the setting sun casting long shadows across the table.

"Do you think they believed the government's story?" Sarah asked quietly, her fingers tracing patterns on the tabletop. "The other kids, I mean."

Alex shrugged. "Maybe. Most of them probably didn't think twice about it. People don't like to ask questions when the answers might scare them."

She nodded, her brow furrowed. "I can't stop thinking about that creature. The way it looked at us..."

"I know," Alex said, his voice low. "But we're going to figure this out. We have to."

Moments later, the pizza arrived, a steaming masterpiece temporarily distracting everyone from their worries. Max and Jam abandoned the arcade to join them, and Logan slid into the booth last, his expression unreadable as he grabbed a slice.

"Alright," Max said through a mouthful of pizza. "Let's just... go over this again. We saw a giant explosion, weird government dudes in hazmat suits, and a monster out of a nightmare. And now they want us to believe it was all a 'minor accident.'"

"Pretty much," Logan said flatly.

"I'm telling you, they're hiding something huge," Jam added, wiping his hands on a napkin. "Those recordings I got? They weren't random. They were signals, and they were coming from Helix Labs."

Sarah's eyes widened. "You're saying they knew this would happen?"

"Or they caused it," Jam replied, his voice grim.

The table fell silent, the weight of his words settling over them. Outside, the neon sign flickered again, casting eerie flashes of red and green across the parking lot.

"So, what do we do?" Sarah asked.

Alex took a deep breath, glancing around at his friends. They all looked back at him, waiting for a plan. "We keep digging," he said finally. "We discover what they're hiding and why that thing was after us. But most importantly, we stick together. No matter what."

Max raised his soda. "To sticking together," he said with a grin.

The others also raised their drinks. In the corner, the arcade machines beeped and whirred, the sounds almost drowning out the faint buzz of tension lingering in the air. They had pizza, friendship, and a momentary sense of safety for now, but they all knew the calm wouldn't last.

Chapter 2: The New Kid

The school bus stopped before Shadowridge High, and Logan stepped off, his combat boots crunching against the gravel. Despite having been in town for a few months, the uneasy stares from his classmates hadn't stopped. He adjusted the strap of his black backpack, which was weighed down with textbooks and a new pack of Magic: The Gathering cards he'd picked up over the weekend. Today, the tension in the air wasn't directed at him but felt thicker than usual—a reminder of the black vans parked just a few blocks away.

Logan glanced at the school's entrance. Students milled about in small clusters, some whispering nervously. The aftermath of the assembly lingered in every hallway and classroom. Word had spread fast about the "incident" at Helix Labs, and while the government's explanation might have calmed some, it had only raised more questions for Logan and his new group of friends.

Inside the building, Logan spotted Alex leaning against his locker, his expression as grim as ever. Jamari and Sarah stood nearby, Sarah clutching her binder like a shield while Jam scrolled through something on his clunky PDA.

"Mornin'," Logan greeted, his tone calm. "Everyone still alive after yesterday?"

Max appeared from around the corner, a bag of Skittles in hand. "Barely," he said, popping a handful into his mouth. "Pretty sure I dreamed about that creature last night. Not fun."

"I'd rather dream about it than run into it again," Sarah muttered. She glanced nervously down the hallway where a pair of suited agents—different from the ones at the assembly—were standing near the principal's office. Their presence was a stark reminder of how close the group had come to real danger.

"So, what's the plan?" Jamari asked, shoving the PDA into his backpack. "Do we just keep pretending we're normal kids while we figure this out, or...?"

"We keep our heads down," Alex said firmly, crossing his arms. "At least until we know more about what's going on. The last thing we need is those agents connecting us to Helix Labs."

"Good luck with that," Logan said. He nodded toward the agents, now speaking to Principal Reynolds with matching frowns. "Something tells me they're not here to check the lunch menu."

The day dragged on, the monotony of classes a sharp contrast to the tension bubbling under the surface. By lunchtime, the group had regrouped at their usual table in the far corner of the cafeteria. It was quieter than usual, many students casting wary glances at the agents who lingered near the faculty lounge.

"Did you guys hear about Jake Pritchard?" Max asked, his voice low. "His parents pulled him out of school this morning. Packed up and left town."

Sarah's eyes widened. "Jake? Why?"

Max shrugged. "No clue. Rumor has it the agents went to his house last night. Bet it's connected to all this Helix Labs stuff."

"Great," Logan said dryly. "So now they're just making people disappear? That's comforting."

"We don't know that for sure," Alex said, though his tone wasn't convincing. He glanced toward the agents, his jaw tightening. "But it's another reason to stay under the radar."

Jamari leaned forward, his voice barely above a whisper. "I've been digging through old newspaper archives. I found some articles about Helix Labs from when it was still active. There were... incidents. Accidents that never made the front page. People went missing back then, too."

The group exchanged uneasy looks, the weight of Jamari's words settling over them. Whatever was happening now clearly had deep roots in Shadowridge's past.

After school, the group decided to meet at the old barn on the edge of town, a secluded spot they'd claimed as their unofficial headquarters where they met when they couldn't meet at Sarah's. The ride there was tense, the late afternoon sun casting long shadows over the narrow dirt road. By the time they arrived, the barn's weathered wood and creaking doors felt almost welcoming compared to the eerie events of the past few days.

Alex pushed the doors open, revealing the familiar interior: a makeshift table made from an old door, mismatched chairs, and a pile of blankets in the corner where they'd sometimes camp out on summer nights.

"Alright," Alex said, dropping his backpack onto the table. "What do we know so far?"

"We know the government's lying," Logan said, sitting cross-legged on a hay bale. "And we know that creature... thing... whatever it is, wasn't just some random accident."

"They called it a subject," Jamari added. "Like it was part of an experiment."

"An experiment that got loose," Sarah said, her voice shaky. "And now they're trying to cover it up."

Alex nodded. "Which means we need to figure out what else they're hiding. Jam, can you keep digging? Old files, anything you can find on Helix Labs."

"Already on it," Jamari said with a determined nod.

"What about us?" Max asked. "What do we do while Jam plays hacker?"

"We stay alert," Alex said. "Anything strange, anything out of place, we note it. And we stay out of sight. The last thing we need is those agents sniffing around here."

The group murmured their agreement, though the unease was palpable. As the sun dipped below the horizon, painting the barn in shades of orange and purple, the reality of their situation felt heavier than ever. Whatever secrets Helix Labs held, they were getting closer to uncovering them—and closer to the danger that came with knowing the truth.

The wind picked up as the group settled into the barn, rustling the rafters and adding an unsettling undertone to the conversation. Despite the familiar setting, the weight of what they'd witnessed—and what they were up against—loomed large.

Max leaned back on his chair, balancing it precariously on two legs. "So, we're just supposed to wait around and hope Jam's hacker skills save the day? Sounds... safe."

"It's not about waiting," Alex said, pacing near the makeshift table. "It's about being smart. If we act like nothing happened and keep a low profile, we'll have time to figure this out without tipping off the agents."

"Assuming they don't already know we're involved," Logan pointed out. He fiddled with a loose thread on his jacket, his eyes distant. "We're kids. How long do you think we can stay under their radar?"

"Long enough," Jamari said, his voice confident despite the tension. He pulled a stack of printouts from his backpack and spread them across the table. "I started pulling everything I could find about Helix Labs. Old articles, government filings, and even conspiracy theory blogs. Some of it's junk, but there's a pattern if you look close enough."

Sarah leaned forward, studying the papers. "What kind of pattern?"

"Disappearances," Jamari replied, pointing to a timeline he'd scribbled on a notebook page. "People who worked at Helix Labs, nearby residents... they've been vanishing for years. And not just back when the lab was active. This stuff keeps happening, even after they shut it down."

"So whatever's going on there never really stopped," Alex said, his tone grim. "They just buried it."

"And now it's unburied," Max added. "Awesome."

Logan's gaze flicked toward the barn door as though expecting someone to burst in at any moment. "What about that thing we saw? The creature. Did you find anything about that?"

Jamari hesitated. "Not directly. But there are mentions of... experiments. Stuff that's way outside the realm of normal science. Genetic manipulation, energy fields, even some kind of dimensional research."

Sarah's face paled. "Dimensional research? Like... other dimensions?"

"That's what it sounds like," Jamari said. "But there's no solid proof. Just rumors and fragments. Whatever they were doing, it's way beyond anything you'd find in a high school science textbook."

"Great," Max muttered. "So, we're dealing with mad scientists, shadowy government guys, and a monster from another dimension. No big deal."

Alex stopped pacing and placed his hands on the table, leaning in. "We're not running from this," he said firmly. If we don't figure out what's happening, more people will get hurt—maybe worse."

The group fell silent, the enormity of the situation sinking in. Outside, the wind howled, rattling the barn's old windows.

"Alright," Logan said finally, his tone resigned but determined. "What's the next move?"

Jamari shuffled through his papers, pulling out a grainy photocopy of a map. "I found this in an old article. It's a layout of the Helix Labs site from before it was shut down. If we're going to figure out what's happening, we must get back there."

"Back there?" Sarah's voice rose an octave. "Are you serious? After what we saw? That... that thing could still be out there!"

"It's risky," Alex admitted. "But if Jam's right, the answers are at Helix Labs. We'll plan it carefully. Go at night, avoid the agents, and get out fast."

Sarah looked unconvinced but didn't argue further. Max, surprisingly, nodded. "Alright, let's do it. But if I get eaten by a monster, I'm haunting you guys forever."

"Deal," Logan said with a faint smirk.

They spent the next hour poring over the map and planning their approach. By the time they left the barn, the sun had set, and the sky was a deep, star-speckled black. As they pedaled home, the tension in the air felt heavier than ever. They were heading straight into danger, but none of them could shake the feeling that they had no choice.

The following night arrived quickly, cloaked in heavy darkness that seemed to settle over Shadowridge whenever the winds shifted. The group agreed to meet at the old railroad tracks just outside town, a secluded spot they'd used for late-night rendezvous. Alex arrived first, his flashlight cutting through the gloom as he waited for the others to appear.

"Are you sure about this?" Sarah's voice broke through the stillness as she approached, her bike's tires crunching against the gravel. Her apprehension was evident in how she clutched the flashlight's handle, her knuckles white.

"We have to be," Alex replied. "If there's something dangerous out there, we can't ignore it."

Jamari arrived next, followed closely by Max and Logan, who carried an old crowbar he'd swiped from his family's shed. "Just in case," he muttered, noticing Alex's questioning glance. The group exchanged a few nervous words before setting off toward the overgrown path that led to Helix Labs.

When they arrived, the ruins of Helix Labs were eerily quiet. The charred remains of the explosion were still visible, but the site seemed even more foreboding in the dark. Jamari unfolded the map, using the light from his PDA to illuminate its faded lines.

"If we're looking for answers, the lab's lower levels are our best bet," Jamari said, pointing to a section labeled "Research and Containment."

"Containment?" Max asked, his voice trembling slightly. "That's... comforting."

"Stick close," Alex said, taking the lead. They moved cautiously through the rubble, avoiding the beams of flashlights in the distance—the agents still patrolling the area.

Sarah froze as they crept closer to the remnants of the main building. "Did you hear that?" she whispered.

The group halted, straining to listen. At first, there was nothing but the distant hum of the agents' equipment. Then, a faint sound reached their ears: a rhythmic, almost mechanical breathing. It came from a collapsed wall section near what had once been the loading docks.

"We shouldn't be here," Sarah said, stepping back.

"That's exactly why we must be here," Alex countered, his flashlight beam sweeping over the debris. "Stay together."

The breathing grew louder as they approached. When Alex's flashlight landed on the source of the sound, the group collectively gasped. Amid the rubble was a figure—humanlike but unmistakably different. The being was curled up, arms wrapped around its knees, and pale skin shimmered faintly under the light. Its eyes opened suddenly, glowing faintly in the darkness.

"What the hell is that?" Logan whispered, gripping the crowbar tightly.

"It's... scared," Sarah said softly, taking a hesitant step forward. Despite her fear, she couldn't ignore how the creature's gaze darted between them, its expression wary and vulnerable.

The mutant flinched as Sarah's flashlight beam moved closer, raising a hand to shield its face. Its voice was soft and halting when it spoke, like it struggled to form words. "No... harm..."

The group exchanged wide-eyed looks. Jamari's grip on his PDA tightened. "It... it can talk?"

"What are you?" Alex asked cautiously, lowering his flashlight slightly. "Do you have a name?"

The mutant hesitated, its eyes flickering with an unreadable emotion. "Name... no name. Number." It gestured weakly toward itself. "MW... three... seven... four... six."

"That's not a name," Sarah said gently. "That's a number."

"Helix... gave... number," the mutant said, its voice growing fainter. It swayed slightly as though the effort of speaking was too much.

"We can't leave it here," Sarah said, looking at the others. "It'll die."

"Or it'll kill us," Logan said darkly. But even he didn't sound convinced.

Alex stepped forward, making a decision. "We take it with us. If Helix Labs created it, the agents will probably look for it. We'll figure out the rest later."

Logan groaned but didn't argue further. Together, they carefully helped the mutant out of the rubble. Its movements were weak but cooperative, and it leaned heavily on Alex and Sarah as they returned to the edge of the site. All the while, the glowing eyes of the agents' flashlights swept the distance, oblivious to the escape happening right under their noses.

The group pedaled furiously away from the ruins of Helix Labs, their hearts pounding with adrenaline and fear. The mutant—or MW3746, as she had been called—sat awkwardly in the wagon attached to the back of Jamari's bike. Its glowing eyes darted around as if expecting an ambush at any moment.

When they reached the barn, Alex carefully helped the mutant out of the wagon, and the group gathered around it. The creature sat on a pile of hay, her body tense and wary but no longer trembling.

"Okay," Max said, pacing. "So, we've officially kidnapped a mutant. What's the plan now?"

"First," Alex said, "we figure out what to call her."

"How about 'Creepy Glowy Eyes'?" Max suggested, earning a glare from Sarah.

Sarah crouched down, her voice gentle. "You said Helix Labs gave you a number. MW3746. Is it okay if we give you a name?"

The mutant's glowing eyes softened slightly, and it nodded.

Jamari tapped his chin thoughtfully. "MW3746... if you look at the numbers on a phone keypad, the letters for 3, 7, 4, and 6 spell out 'E-R-I-N.'"

"Erin," Sarah said, testing the name. She smiled at the mutant. "How does that sound?"

The mutant—Erin—tilted her head as though considering the word. Then it nodded again, this time with more certainty. "Erin," she said, her voice still halting but more evident now.

Max shrugged. "Alright, Erin, it is. Welcome to... whatever this is."

Logan leaned against the barn wall, his arms crossed. "Great, now we're naming it. Next, we'll probably build a room and get it a birthday cake."

"Logan," Alex said sharply, "we're just trying to make her feel safe. You saw how scared she was back there."

Logan rolled his eyes but didn't argue further. Instead, he watched as Erin's gaze flicked between the group as though trying to piece together who they were.

"Erin," Sarah said gently, "can you tell us anything about Helix Labs? Why were they keeping you there?"

Erin hesitated, its expression shifting to one of confusion and pain. It clutched at its head, letting out a soft whimper.

"It's okay," Alex said quickly, raising his hands in a calming gesture. "You don't have to talk about it if it's too hard."

Erin relaxed slightly, though its hands still trembled. "Bad place," she said softly. "They... made me. Wanted... control."

The group exchanged uneasy glances.

"Made you?" Jamari asked cautiously. "Like an experiment?"

Erin nodded. "Not... alone. Others, too. Gone now."

"Gone where?" Sarah pressed, her voice trembling.

Erin's glowing eyes dimmed slightly. "Lost. Taken. Dead."

The barn fell silent, the weight of Erin's words pressing down like a heavy blanket.

"This is worse than we thought," Alex said finally. "If there were others, and they... didn't make it, that means whatever Helix Labs was doing, it's way bigger than Erin."

"Which means we're way in over our heads," Logan muttered.

"Maybe," Sarah said, her voice steadier now, "but we can't just abandon Erin. If we don't help, who will?"

"She's right," Alex agreed. "We're in this now, whether we like it or not."

Max sighed, flopping onto a hay bale. "Man, I miss when our biggest problem was finding enough quarters for the arcade."

The faintest hint of a smile flickered across Erin's face, and for a moment, the tension eased. But the reality of their situation remained stark. They had no idea what they were up against, and the shadows of Helix Labs loomed more significant than ever.

The night stretched on as the group sat in the barn, their nerves frayed but their determination solidifying. Erin had fallen into an uneasy sleep, curled up on the hay with a blanket draped over her. The group huddled around the makeshift table, whispering to avoid waking her.

"So, what's the plan?" Logan asked, his voice low. "We can't hide her here forever."

"We're not even sure what we're hiding her from," Sarah replied. "The agents? Helix Labs? Whatever that thing was back at the site?"

"All of the above," Alex said. "Until we know more, we can't take any chances. Jam, you said you found something about Helix Labs' old experiments?"

Jamari nodded, spreading out more papers and clippings. "There's a mention of something called Project Rift. It's vague, but they were trying to open... portals or dimensions. Erin might be connected to that."

"Portals?" Max whispered, his eyes wide. "Like other worlds?"

"Maybe," Jamari said. "But if that's what they were doing, it'd explain a lot. Like why the government's so desperate to keep this quiet."

"And why Erin's so scared," Sarah added. "If they made her as part of some experiment, they probably treated her like... like a thing, not a person."

Alex's jaw tightened. "Well, she's not a thing. She's one of us now. And we're going to protect her."

"Protect her with what?" Logan asked, gesturing toward the barn door. "We can barely protect ourselves if those agents find us. And if there's more of... whatever that creature was..."

"We'll figure it out," Alex said firmly. "One step at a time."

The group fell into a contemplative silence, their situation weighing on them. Outside, the wind had settled, leaving the barn eerily quiet. Sarah glanced over at Erin, her expression softening.

"She trusted us enough to come with us," Sarah said. "That means something. We can't let her down."

"Agreed," Alex said. He stood, brushing the hay off his jeans. "Let's call it a night. We'll meet back here tomorrow after school and figure out our next move."

The following day brought a tentative calm, though the group's nerves remained on edge. The agents were still present at school, their watchful eyes constantly reminding them of the danger lurking beneath the surface.

Alex, Sarah, Jamari, Logan, and Max huddled at their usual table, speaking in hushed tones during lunch.

"She's stable for now," Sarah reported. "I checked on her this morning before coming to school. She's still really weak, though."

"We need more information," Jamari said. "If Project Rift is the key to all this, we must figure out exactly what it is. I'll dig deeper tonight."

"We should split up after school," Alex suggested. "Jam, keep researching. Sarah and I will check the library for anything about Helix Labs. Max and Logan stock up on supplies. Food, water, anything Erin might need to recover."

"What about keeping an eye on the agents?" Logan asked. "If they're sniffing around too close to the barn, we need to know."

Alex nodded. "Good point. Max, think you can handle that?"

Max gave a mock salute. "On it, boss."

As the group's makeshift plan began to take shape, the bell rang, signaling the end of lunch. They filed out of the cafeteria, their movements deliberate and their minds buzzing with purpose. Their quiet resolve was clear: they were in this together, no matter what.

Alex couldn't shake the feeling that they were being watched as they moved through the halls. He glanced over his shoulder, catching sight of an unfamiliar figure standing near the principal's office. The man wasn't wearing a suit like the other agents. Instead, he was dressed in plain clothes, his sharp gaze fixed on Alex for a moment too long before he turned away.

Alex's stomach churned. He didn't say anything to the others, but the nagging thought lingered: the agents weren't the only ones watching them. Something else was coming, and they had to be ready.

Chapter 3: Whispers in the Woods

The early evening sky was painted orange and purple as the group reconvened at the barn. Erin sat quietly in the corner, her glowing eyes watching them with curiosity and apprehension. Her recovery was slow, and though she was speaking more, her fragmented sentences left much unsaid.

Alex unfolded the map of Shadowridge, smoothing it across the makeshift table. "We need to figure out what the agents are looking for. Whatever they're hunting, it's tied to Erin, Helix Labs, and that creature."

Jamari tapped a pen against the map, circling the woods near Helix Labs. "The sightings from the old newspaper articles I found all cluster around this area. Strange lights, noises, even a few disappearances. If we're going to find answers, that's where we start."

Sarah glanced at Erin. "Do you know anything about the woods?" she asked gently.

Erin's eyes flickered. "Dark... cold. Home... once," she murmured. Her hands fidgeted with the edge of the blanket draped over her shoulders.

"Home?" Logan asked, his brow furrowing. "What does that mean?"

Erin didn't answer, her gaze shifting to the floor. The group exchanged uneasy glances.

"Alright," Alex said, folding the map. "We'll head out tonight. Stay together, stay quiet, and watch for anything unusual."

The forest felt alive as they entered, the faint rustling of leaves and distant hoots of owls creating an almost hypnotic backdrop. The moonlight filtered through the canopy, casting long, twisted shadows that seemed to move with a mind of their own. Erin walked beside Sarah, her movements hesitant but purposeful.

"This place is creepy even without the government conspiracies," Max muttered, gripping his flashlight tightly. "Why do all the weird things have to happen in the woods?"

"Because it's Shadowridge," Jamari replied, scanning the area with a hand-held EMF reader he'd rigged together. "Weird is practically the town motto."

Logan stopped suddenly, holding up a hand. "Wait. Do you hear that?"

The group froze, straining to listen. At first, there was only the rustle of leaves in the breeze. Then, faintly, a low, guttural growl echoed through the trees.

"What the hell was that?" Max whispered, his voice shaky.

Erin's glowing eyes flared brighter, and she clutched Sarah's arm. "Not safe," she said urgently. "They... watch."

"Who watches?" Alex asked, stepping closer to Erin.

Before she could answer, the growl came again, louder this time. Branches snapped in the distance, and the underbrush rustled violently. The group huddled together, their flashlights darting across the shadows.

"Run," Erin whispered, her voice trembling.

"What?" Sarah asked.

"Run!" Erin screamed, her voice ringing in the stillness.

The group turned and bolted without hesitation, their feet pounding against the forest floor. The sound of pursuit followed them—heavy, rapid footfalls and the snapping of branches. Alex glanced back, his flashlight beam catching a brief glimpse of something massive and hunched, its glowing eyes eerily similar to Erin's but filled with malice.

"This way!" Alex shouted, veering toward a break in the trees. The group followed, their breaths coming in gasps as they sprinted through the dense woods. Erin stumbled, and Sarah caught her, pulling her forward.

"Don't stop!" Sarah urged.

They burst into a small clearing, the moonlight illuminating an old, dilapidated structure resembling a hunting cabin.

"In there!" Logan yelled.

The group scrambled inside, slamming the door shut behind them. The cabin smelled of damp wood and mildew; the only light came from their flashlights. Alex braced the door with a heavy beam, his chest heaving.

"Is everyone okay?" he asked, his voice shaking.

"Define okay," Max replied, collapsing onto an old chair.

Erin stood near the center of the room, her eyes glowing softly in the dark. She seemed calmer now, but her hands still trembled.

"What was that thing?" Logan demanded, his voice sharp. "Was it another experiment?"

Erin hesitated, then nodded. "Same... but not. Strong. Angry."

"Angry at what?" Sarah asked gently.

"Me," Erin said, her voice barely audible.

The group exchanged uneasy glances. Outside, the sounds of the forest began to quiet, but the tension in the cabin remained thick.

"We need a new plan," Alex said finally. "Whatever that thing is, it's not going to stop. And we're not leaving this forest without some answers."

The group huddled in the cabin, their flashlights creating shifting shadows on the warped wooden walls. Erin sat in the corner, her glowing eyes dimmed as if exhausted from the encounter. Sarah knelt beside her, offering her a bottle of water. Erin took it hesitantly, her trembling hands making the bottle wobble.

"Hey," Sarah said softly, trying to meet Erin's gaze. "It's okay now. We're safe in here."

Erin's glowing eyes briefly flickered up to meet Sarah's before she nodded. "Safe... for now," she said, her voice barely audible.

Max paced near the door, his usual levity replaced by a nervous energy. "Did anyone else see how fast that thing was? It was like a freaking freight train with claws!"

"And it was after Erin," Logan added, leaning against the wall with his arms crossed. "Why? What does it want from her?"

Erin flinched at Logan's tone, and Sarah shot him a sharp glare. "Logan, stop. She's been through enough without you interrogating her."

"I'm not interrogating," Logan replied, his voice softer but still wary. "I'm just saying we need answers. We're putting our necks on the line here."

"And we'll figure it out together," Alex interjected, his voice firm. He sat down cross-legged on the floor, facing Erin. "Erin, can you tell us anything about that thing? Why it's after you?"

Erin hesitated, her fingers twisting the blanket's hem around her shoulders. "It... knows me," she said finally. "Like me... but not. Helix... made it."

"Made it like they made you?" Jamari asked, his curiosity evident despite the tension.

Erin nodded. "Same place. Same pain. But it... broke. Angry. Only anger now."

The weight of her words hung in the air, and for a moment, no one spoke. Max finally broke the silence, his voice quieter than usual. "So, it's like your evil twin?"

Sarah shot him another glare, but Erin surprised them all by giving a small, faint smile. "Not twin," she said. "Shadow."

"A shadow of you," Alex mused. "That... makes sense. If it came from the same experiments, it might see you as part of why it's in so much pain."

"Or it's just a mindless monster," Logan said grimly. "Either way, it's not going to stop."

"Which is why we have to figure out a way to stop it," Alex said. He looked at Jamari. "You said you found something about Project Rift? Could it help?"

Jamari pulled his PDA from his bag, scrolling through his notes. "Maybe. If this thing is connected to whatever dimensional stuff Helix was messing with, there might be a way to... I don't know. Should I serve the connection or shut it down?"

"That's a big maybe," Logan pointed out.

"It's all we've got right now," Alex countered. He turned back to Erin. "Do you remember anything about Project Rift? Anything at all?"

Erin's brow furrowed as she seemed to search her fragmented memories. "Door," she said finally. "They called it... a door to somewhere else. But it wasn't safe. Broke things. Broke minds."

The group exchanged uneasy glances. Sarah reached out, placing a comforting hand on Erin's shoulder. "We'll help you figure this out," she said softly. "You're not alone anymore."

Erin's glowing eyes met Sarah's, and for the first time, a spark of trust seemed to flicker in her expression. "Not alone," she echoed, her voice steadier.

"Alright," Alex said, standing. "We regroup tomorrow and figure out our next step. We stay here until it's safe to head back."

As the group settled in for the night, their bond felt more potent. Despite the danger and the unknowns, they had one another—and now, they had Erin, too. For the first time, the fear felt manageable. Together, they might have a chance.

The dawn crept over Shadowridge, its soft light spilling across the quiet streets as the group cautiously returned to town. Erin walked close to Sarah, her tattered, ill-fitting clothing and cautious gait drawing the occasional curious glance from early risers. Max lagged slightly behind, nervously scanning their surroundings for signs of the shadow creature or government agents.

"Relax, Max," Logan muttered, though his eyes were just as watchful. "We're not exactly inconspicuous, but they won't come after us in broad daylight."

"Unless they're desperate," Max replied, quickening his pace to keep up with the others.

Sarah glanced over at Erin, whose pale skin and glowing eyes stood out starkly against the morning sun. "First things first," she said. "We need to get you something more normal to wear. My house isn't far. We'll figure something out there."

Erin tilted her head, her expression unreadable. "Normal?" she echoed softly as though the word was foreign.

Sarah smiled gently. "Clothes that blend in. Something comfortable. You'll like it, I promise."

When they arrived at Sarah's house, the group filed quietly, careful not to wake her parents. The house was spacious but cozy, filled with the faint smell of lavender and sunlight streaming through lace curtains. Sarah led Erin up the stairs to her room, where a mix of posters, books, and neatly folded clothes revealed her tidy yet creative personality.

"Here," Sarah said, opening her closet. "Let's see if anything fits you."

Erin stood awkwardly in the center of the room, her eyes darting between the colorful garments. "Why?" she asked.

Sarah paused, turning to face Erin. "Because you deserve to have nice things. You're part of our group now. And... it'll help you feel more like yourself."

Erin hesitated, her fingers brushing over the fabric of a soft sweater. "Self?" she repeated as though testing the word.

"Yeah," Sarah said, pulling the sweater and holding it out. "Yourself. Who you are, not what Helix Labs tried to make you. Come on, try it."

Erin took the sweater slowly, her glowing eyes flickering with curiosity and uncertainty. She turned it over in her hands and looked back at Sarah. "You... help?"

Sarah grinned. "Of course. That's what friends are for."

The rest of the group waited downstairs in the living room. Max flipped through the TV channels, stopping on a local news report. The headline read: *Government Continues Investigation Into Helix Labs Incident.*

"You've gotta be kidding me," Max muttered, increasing the volume. The reporter stood in front of the charred remains of Helix Labs, gesturing toward a group of agents in the background.

"Officials have assured the public that there is no immediate danger," the reporter said, "but questions remain about the cause of the explosion and the rumored containment breach. Residents are urged to report any suspicious activity."

Logan groaned. "Great. So, if anyone sees Erin, they're supposed to call those guys?"

Alex leaned forward, his expression grim. "It just means we have to be even more careful. We can't let her out of sight until we figure out what to do next."

At that moment, Sarah and Erin descended the stairs. Erin wore the sweater Sarah had picked out and slightly too-big jeans, which still improved over her previous outfit. Her glowing eyes seemed less intense, as though the change in clothes had softened her presence.

"Well?" Sarah asked, looking at the group.

Max gave a thumbs-up. "Much better. You're practically a regular Shadowridge kid now."

Erin's lips quirked upward in what might have been a smile. "Shadowridge... kid," she said quietly, as though trying the words on for size.

Sarah beamed. "See? I told you you'd like it."

The moment of levity was short-lived as Alex pointed toward the TV. "They're ramping up their search," he said, nodding toward the broadcast. "We must figure out our next move before they get too close."

"And before that thing comes back," Logan added darkly.

Erin's expression faltered, her gaze dropping to the floor. Sarah stepped closer, placing a reassuring hand on her shoulder. "We'll keep you safe," she said firmly. "No matter what."

Erin nodded, though the uncertainty in her eyes remained. For now, all they could do was prepare for what lay ahead.

By late afternoon, the group decided Erin needed a proper introduction to their favorite hangout spot: the Pizza Palace. The familiar neon sign buzzed faintly above the door as they locked their bikes outside. Erin's glowing eyes dimmed slightly, her nervousness apparent as they entered the bustling restaurant.

"Relax," Sarah said, giving her a reassuring smile. "You're going to love this place."

Inside, the aroma of melted cheese and pepperoni mingled with the sounds of clinking arcade machines. Max was the first to dart toward the counter, ordering their usual: a large pepperoni pizza with extra cheese.

"You gotta try the pizza here," Max told Erin, grinning. "It'll change your life."

Erin watched as the group slid into their usual booth near the arcade. She sat stiffly between Sarah and Alex, her glowing eyes scanning the room with curiosity and apprehension. Jamari slid a quarter across the table toward her.

"You ever play pinball?" he asked, nodding toward the nearby machine.

Erin picked up the coin and examined it closely. "Play?" she echoed, tilting her head.

"Yeah," Jamari said with a grin. "Come on, I'll show you."

As Jamari guided Erin to the pinball machine, the rest of the group settled into the booth. Alex kept a watchful eye on the entrance, his unease growing. "We should keep this quick," he said. "I don't like being out in the open like this."

"You worry too much," Max replied, spinning a quarter on the table. "No one here's paying attention to us."

But Max's words proved to be overly optimistic. A group of older teens approached, their sneering expressions instantly putting the group on edge. Travis was at the front of the pack, a local troublemaker notorious for picking fights.

"Well, well, what do we have here?" Travis drawled, leaning against their booth. "The nerd squad... and a new freak. Where'd you find her? The circus?"

Alex stood up, his fists clenched. "Leave us alone, Travis."

"Or what?" Travis sneered. "You gonna hit me, hero?"

Sarah grabbed Alex's arm. "Don't," she whispered. "It's not worth it."

But Travis wasn't done. He turned toward Erin, who was now standing beside Jamari. Her glowing eyes widened as he stepped closer. "What's with her eyes? That's not normal. You guys keeping secrets?"

"Back off, Travis," Logan said, stepping between him and Erin. "I'm serious."

"Make me," Travis shot back.

The confrontation quickly escalated. When Erin backed away, her fear palpable, Travis laughed mockingly. "What's the matter, freak? Are you afraid of a little fun?"

Erin's breathing grew shallow. To her, the aggressive teens were no different than the agents who had tormented her. Panic took hold, and her glowing eyes flared brightly.

"No!" she shouted, raising her hands instinctively.

Before anyone could react, Erin's energy pulse exploded, rippling through the room like an unseen wave. The arcade machines flickered wildly, their lights surging before shorting out completely. Tables and chairs skidded across the floor, and Travis and his friends were thrown backward, crashing into the wall.

The entire restaurant fell silent, patrons frozen in shock as the lights dimmed. Erin stood trembling in the center of the chaos, her hands still raised and her glowing eyes fading to their usual dim hue.

"Erin, stop!" Alex shouted, rushing to her side. He placed his hands on her shoulders, trying to steady her. "It's okay. You're okay."

Erin blinked rapidly as though coming out of a trance. She looked at Alex, her face crumpling with guilt. "I... didn't mean..." she stammered.

"We need to go," Logan said urgently, helping Sarah and Jamari gather their things. "Now."

The group bolted out of the Pizza Palace, leaving stunned onlookers and a mess of overturned furniture. Travis and his friends groaned, too dazed to follow.

As they pedaled away into the twilight, Erin sat in the wagon behind Jamari's bike, her head bowed low. Sarah glanced back at her, her heart aching at Erin's distress.

"It's not your fault," Sarah called over her shoulder. "You were scared. We'll figure this out, okay?"

Erin didn't respond, but Alex gave Sarah a nod of gratitude. The group veered off the main road, heading toward the safety of the woods. The distant glow of the Pizza Palace faded behind them, leaving only the sounds of their wheels crunching on gravel and the faint rustle of the trees ahead.

Chapter 4: Shadows in Pursuit

The group's bikes skidded to a halt at the edge of the woods, the air still buzzing with tension from the incident at the Pizza Palace. Erin stepped out of the wagon, her shoulders hunched as if trying to shrink herself from view. Her glowing eyes darted nervously between the trees and flinched at every sound.

Alex looked around, his flashlight casting sharp beams through the encroaching darkness. "We'll hide out here for now," he said, his voice firm but calm. "We can't go back into town until we figure out what to do."

"Hide?" Erin whispered, her voice trembling. "I... hurt them."

Sarah stepped forward, placing a reassuring hand on Erin's arm. "You didn't mean to," she said gently. "You were scared. Anyone would have been."

"She's right," Jamari added. "But we've got bigger problems now. People saw what happened. If the agents weren't suspicious, they would be all over us after this."

"And Travis and his goons aren't going to keep their mouths shut," Logan muttered, crossing his arms. "They'll probably twist the story into something worse."

Max sat down on a fallen log, running a hand through his hair. "Great. So now we've got bullies, government agents, and a killer monster all breathing down our necks. This keeps getting better."

"Let's focus," Alex said sharply. He turned to Jamari. "You've been researching Project Rift. Any chance it's connected to Erin's powers?"

Jamari pulled out his PDA and began scrolling through his notes. "It's possible. I've found that Project Rift wasn't just about opening doors to other dimensions and controlling what came through. If Erin and that shadow thing are tied to it, they might be byproducts of whatever Helix Labs experimented with."

"So what does that mean for us?" Sarah asked, glancing between Jamari and Alex.

"It means Erin's not just some random experiment," Alex said. "She's part of something bigger. And if the agents want her back that badly, it's because they think she's the key to controlling whatever they unleashed."

Erin's eyes widened. "Key?" she murmured, taking a step back. "No. Not a key. Don't want... them."

"And they're not getting you," Alex said firmly. "We're going to protect you, no matter what."

Erin's gaze softened slightly, but the fear in her expression didn't fully fade.

As the group ventured deeper into the woods, the trees closed around them, their gnarled branches forming a canopy blocking the moonlight. Jamari's EMF reader began to beep faintly, and he frowned as he examined the device.

"Something's nearby," he said. "It's faint, but it's not normal."

"Define 'not normal,'" Max said, his voice tinged with nervous energy.

Before Jamari could answer, a distant rustling sound echoed through the woods. The group froze, their eyes scanning the darkness. The sound grew louder, accompanied by a low growl that made the hairs on the back of Alex's neck stand up.

"It's back," Logan said grimly, gripping the crowbar he'd brought from the barn.

"Run," Alex ordered, his voice steady despite the panic surging. "Stick together and head for the creek. It'll slow it down."

The group took off, their feet pounding against the forest floor as the growling grew closer. Erin stumbled, and Sarah grabbed her arm, pulling her forward. "Come on! You can do this!" she urged.

The shadow creature burst through the trees, its glowing eyes locking onto the group. It moved with terrifying speed, its elongated limbs slicing through the underbrush. Max glanced back, his face pale. "It's gaining on us!"

Alex spotted the creek ahead, its shallow waters glinting faintly in the darkness. "This way!" he shouted, leading the group down the bank. They splashed through the water, the cold seeping into their shoes, but they didn't stop.

When they reached the other side, Alex turned, grabbing a heavy branch as a makeshift weapon. The creature stopped at the creek's edge, its glowing eyes narrowing. For a moment, it seemed hesitant, its gaze shifting to Erin.

Erin stepped forward, her trembling hands raising slightly. "Stop," she said, her voice soft but firm. "Go... away."

The creature growled, its body tensing as if preparing to attack. But then Erin's eyes flared brighter, and a pulse of energy rippled through the air. The creature recoiled, its form flickering like a shadow caught in the wind. With a final, guttural snarl, it turned and disappeared into the trees.

The group stood in stunned silence, their breaths coming in ragged gasps. Sarah stepped closer to Erin, her voice filled with awe. "How did you do that?"

Erin shook her head, her glowing eyes dimming once more. "Don't know. Just... felt it."

Alex lowered the branch, his hands still shaking. "Whatever you did, it worked. But we can't stay here. If it comes back..."

Jamari nodded, his expression serious. "We need a plan. A real one. If that thing's tied to Project Rift, we must figure out how to stop it for good."

"And keep Erin safe," Sarah added, her voice unwavering.

Alex looked at the group, their faces illuminated by the faint glow of Erin's eyes. Despite their fear and exhaustion, their expressions matched his determination.

"Then let's get to work," he said. Together, they turned and began making their way deeper into the woods, the shadows pressing around them as the fight for answers and survival continued.

The forest became darker, and the deeper they ventured into it, the more tense the air was. Every rustle of leaves and snap of a twig set their nerves on edge. Erin clung to Sarah's side, her eyes glowing faintly as though attuned to every shadow around them.

"We need to find shelter," Alex said, his voice steady despite his heart pounding. "Something defensible."

"The old ranger station," Jamari suggested, glancing at his PDA, which now functioned as a makeshift map. "It's about a mile north from here. No one's used it in years, but it should still stand."

"And if it's not?" Logan asked, gripping the crowbar tightly.

"Then we'll figure it out," Alex replied firmly. "Let's move."

The group pressed on, their footsteps muffled by the thick carpet of pine needles. Max tried to lighten the mood, but his voice sounded a low murmur. "You know, this is exactly how every bad horror movie starts. Creepy woods, no way out... all we're missing is the guy with the chain-saw."

"Not helping, Max," Sarah muttered, though her lips twitched in a faint smile.

The sound of rushing water broke through the stillness as they reached a narrow creek. The group paused, scanning their surroundings. Erin's gaze lingered on the water, her expression thoughtful.

"Safe here," she murmured, her voice barely audible.

Alex turned to her. "Why do you think that?"

Erin hesitated as though searching for the right words. "Water... slows them. It's hard to cross. They don't like it."

"Them?" Logan pressed. "You mean the shadow creature?"

Erin nodded slowly, her glowing eyes flickering. "Not just one. More. Watching."

A chill ran through the group as her words sank in. Alex tightened his grip on the makeshift weapon he carried. "We keep moving," he said firmly. "The faster we get to the ranger station, the better."

The ranger station came into view just as the last sliver of twilight faded from the sky. It was small and weathered, with boarded-up windows and a sagging roof, but it was intact. The group approached cautiously, their flashlights sweeping over the structure.

"Looks like it's been abandoned for decades," Jamari said, pushing open the creaking door.

Inside, the air was stale and heavy with the scent of mildew. Dust coated every surface, and cobwebs clung to the corners. An old wood-burning stove stood in one corner, surrounded by rusted tools and a pile of rotting firewood.

"Home sweet home," Max said dryly, brushing cobwebs off a chair and plopping down. "At least it's not crawling with monsters."

"Don't jinx it," Logan muttered, setting his crowbar against the wall.

Alex turned to Erin, who stood near the center of the room, her glowing eyes darting around nervously. "Are you okay?" he asked gently.

Erin's gaze met his, and she nodded slowly. "Safer," she said. "But not safe."

"We'll make it safe," Sarah said, stepping closer to Erin. "We'll figure this out. Together."

As the group settled in, Jamari set up his PDA on the dusty table, using its limited signal to sift through more of the files he'd uncovered about Helix Labs. The others huddled around a small lantern they'd found, its dim light casting eerie shadows on the walls.

"Here," Jamari said, pointing to a grainy blueprint on his screen. "This is part of the original plans for Helix Labs. It mentions a containment chamber beneath the main facility—something they called the Rift Nexus."

"Sounds ominous," Max quipped, leaning over for a better look.

"What's a Rift Nexus?" Sarah asked, frowning.

Jamari shrugged. "Your guess is as good as mine. But if I had to bet, it's where all this started."

Alex's jaw tightened. "Then that's where we're going next. Whatever Helix Labs unleashed, it's tied to that Nexus. If we're going to stop this, we must get inside and shut it down."

"That's a suicide mission," Logan said bluntly. "You saw what's out there. And if there's more than one of those things…"

"Then we find a way to fight them," Alex said firmly. "We're not backing down."

Erin, who had been silent until now, stepped forward. "I… help," she said, her voice quiet but steady.

The group turned to her, their expressions a mix of surprise and concern.

"Erin, you don't have to…" Sarah began, but Erin shook her head.

"They… made me strong," Erin said. "I… want to stop them. Stop… pain."

Alex met her gaze, nodding slowly. "Alright. But we do this together. No one gets left behind."

The group nodded in agreement, their resolve hardening. Outside, the forest remained eerily quiet as though holding its breath. They didn't know what awaited them at the Rift Nexus, but one thing was sure: the fight was far from over.

The silence in the ranger station was oppressive, broken only by the faint hum of Jamari's PDA as he sifted through files. Alex sat at the table, scribbling notes on a scrap of paper, while Logan watched at the window, his crowbar resting against the sill. Erin sat apart from the group, her glowing eyes dimmed as she stared at the dusty floor.

"I found something," Jamari said, his voice cutting through the quiet. "The Rift Nexus wasn't just some random experiment. Helix Labs was trying to tap into a power source from another dimension. Something they called 'The Core.'"

"What kind of power source?" Sarah asked, leaning over his shoulder.

Jamari shook his head. "It's vague, but whatever it is, it's massive. Enough to power cities, maybe even entire regions. But there's a catch..."

"There always is," Logan muttered.

"The Core isn't stable," Jamari continued. "The more they tried to harness it, the more unpredictable it became. That's what caused the original 'containment breach.' And if I'm reading this right, the shadow creatures... they're a byproduct of that instability. They're drawn to the energy."

Max groaned, sliding down the wall until he sat on the floor. "So, not only do we have to deal with monsters, but we're also up against a time bomb from another dimension. Awesome."

Alex tapped his pen against the table, his mind racing. "The Core is still active if the creatures are drawn to the energy. Helix Labs never shut it down."

"And if they're still trying to control it," Sarah added, "that explains why they're so desperate to find Erin. She's connected to the Core somehow."

Erin's head snapped up at her name. "No control," she said firmly. "Not theirs. Not mine."

Alex stood and approached her, crouching to meet her gaze. "We're not going to let them take you. But we need your help to stop them. Do you know anything about shutting the Core down?"

Erin hesitated, her glowing eyes flickering as she struggled to recall. "Core... angry," she murmured. "Needs balance. Too much... breaks things."

"Balance?" Jamari repeated, typing furiously. "That could mean stabilizing the energy flow. If we can figure out how to do that, we might be able to shut it down safely."

"And if we can't?" Logan asked, his tone grim.

"Then we'll have to destroy it," Alex said, his voice hard. "One way or another, this ends."

As the group debated their next steps, the faint sound of approaching footsteps reached Logan's ears. He raised a hand, signaling for silence. "Someone's coming."

The group froze, their eyes darting to the boarded-up windows. The footsteps grew louder, accompanied by the faint murmur of voices. Alex grabbed the crowbar and motioned for the others to stay back.

The voices became more apparent as the intruders drew closer. "Spread out," a man's voice commanded. "Check every building. They're around here somewhere."

"Agents," Sarah whispered, her face pale.

Erin's breathing quickened, and she pressed herself against the wall. "No," she murmured, her voice trembling. "Not again."

"Stay calm," Alex said softly. "We're not going to let them take you."

The group moved quickly, extinguishing their lantern and huddling in the darkest corner. Jamari clutched his PDA, the screen dimmed to avoid detection. The sound of boots crunching against gravel grew louder, stopping outside the ranger station.

"Looks empty," another voice said.

"Check it anyway," the first voice ordered.

A beam of light swept through the cracks in the boarded-up windows, illuminating the dusty interior. Alex gripped the crowbar tightly, his heart pounding as the door creaked open. A flashlight beam darted across the room, stopping short of their hiding spot.

"Clear," the agent called out, stepping back outside.

The group didn't dare move until footsteps faded into the distance. When the coast was clear, Alex let out a shaky breath. "They're getting closer. We can't stay here."

"Then we head for Helix Labs," Sarah said, her voice steady despite the fear in her eyes. "If the Core is the key to stopping this, we don't have a choice."

The group huddled in the ranger station, their minds heavy with the weight of their next move. Alex unfolded Jamari's makeshift map of the Helix Labs site, spreading it across the dusty table. Everyone leaned in, their faces illuminated by the faint glow of Jamari's PDA.

"We don't have many options," Alex began, tracing a finger along the faded blueprint. "If this Nexus is where everything started, then it's where we have to go. But we can't just walk in blind."

"Agreed," Logan said, his tone serious. "We need to know what we're walking into. Erin, can you tell us anything else about what's inside?"

Erin hesitated, her glowing eyes dimming slightly as she searched her fragmented memories. "The Core... strong. Guards it. Not... human. Dangerous."

"Not human?" Max whispered. "As in more of those shadow things?"

Erin nodded solemnly. "And... others. Different."

The group exchanged uneasy glances. Sarah broke the silence, her voice steady despite the fear in her eyes. "We'll face them together. We have to. For Erin. For everyone."

Alex nodded, his resolve hardening. "All right. We'll move at dawn. Get some rest while you can. It's going to be a long day tomorrow."

As the group settled into an uneasy silence, Erin sat with her back against the wall, her glowing eyes dim but focused. She looked at Sarah, her voice soft but sure. "Thank you," she said.

Sarah smiled, squeezing Erin's hand gently. "We're in this together."

Outside, the forest seemed to hold its breath, the shadows deepening as the night stretched. The fight ahead would be their most challenging yet, but together, they carried the faint hope that they could rewrite the ending Helix Labs had tried to script for them all.

The night passed slowly, each of them taking turns keeping watch. Erin sat beside Sarah, her glowing eyes fixed on the faint sliver of moonlight streaming through the boarded windows.

"Afraid," Erin murmured.

Sarah reached over, squeezing her hand gently. "Me too," she admitted. "But we've got each other. We'll get through this. I promise."

Erin's gaze softened, and momentarily, the faintest smile flickered across her face. "Together."

As dawn broke over the horizon, casting the woods in hues of orange and gold, the group prepared to leave. Each packed their little supplies, steeling themselves for the journey ahead. The ranger station faded behind them as they ventured deeper into the forest, the looming silhouette of Helix Labs growing larger with each step.

The shadows seemed to watch their every move, but the group pressed on, their fear outweighed by their determination. The answers—and the battle—awaited them.

Chapter 5: The Descent into Helix Labs

The forest fell silent as the group approached the outer perimeter of Helix Labs. The crumbled remains of the once-imposing facility loomed ahead, bathed in the faint light of the early morning sun. Vines and moss had crept over the cracked walls, nature's reclamation of a place that had harbored unspeakable horrors.

Alex raised a hand, signaling the others to stop. They crouched behind a cluster of overgrown bushes, their breaths visible in the crisp morning air. Jamari pulled out his PDA, the screen flickering faintly as he scanned for nearby signals.

"No active surveillance," Jamari whispered. "At least, nothing obvious."

"That doesn't mean it's safe," Logan muttered, gripping his crowbar tightly. "Stay sharp."

Erin stood slightly apart from the group, her glowing eyes scanning the ruins. Her expression was unreadable, but her hands clenched and unclenched at her sides, a nervous rhythm betraying her tension.

"What's wrong?" Sarah asked, stepping closer to her.

Erin shook her head. "Feels... wrong. Heavy. Like... before."

Alex glanced at her, then back at the facility. "We'll stick to the plan. Get in, find the Nexus, and shut it down. Fast and quiet."

"Quiet," Max repeated, a nervous grin on his face. "Sure. Because that's our style."

The group exchanged faint smiles and a brief moment of fun before the reality of their mission settled over them once more. One by one, they slipped through a gap in the chain-link fence, the rusted metal protesting softly as they passed.

Inside the facility's ruins, the air grew colder, tinged with the faint scent of ozone. Debris littered the ground—shattered glass, twisted metal, and fragments of long-abandoned equipment. Jamari rechecked his PDA, and the device was emitting a faint beep.

"We're close," he said. "There's an access hatch just ahead. It should lead to the lower levels."

"The Nexus," Erin murmured, her voice barely audible. Her glowing eyes flared briefly, reflecting her unease.

The group moved cautiously, every step echoing faintly in the desolate space. They reached the hatch, a heavy metal door partially obscured by rubble. Alex and Logan worked together to clear the debris, their movements deliberate and quiet. Finally, the hatch was revealed, its surface marked with faded warnings and the Helix Labs logo.

"Here goes nothing," Alex said, gripping the wheel and turning it with a grunt of effort. The hatch creaked open, revealing a dark shaft descending into the facility's depths. A faint, pulsing light emanated from below, casting eerie shadows on the walls.

"This is it," Jamari said, his voice a mixture of awe and dread. "The Rift Nexus is down there."

Max peered into the darkness, his usual bravado faltering. "So, uh... who's going first?"

Alex stepped forward, his flashlight cutting through the gloom. "I am. Stay close, and watch each other's backs."

The group descended the narrow ladder one by one, their movements slow and cautious. The air grew warmer the deeper they went, humming with an unnatural energy that made the hairs on their necks stand on end. When they reached the bottom, they found themselves in a wide corridor with flickering fluorescent lights.

"This place still has power?" Logan asked, his voice low.

"Not power," Erin said, her voice distant. "The Core. It... feeds."

The corridor led to a massive steel door, its surface etched with intricate patterns that seemed to shift and shimmer under the flickering lights. Jamari's PDA beeped rapidly, its screen flashing red.

"That's it," he said, pointing to the door. "The Nexus."

"And whatever's guarding it," Logan added grimly.

Alex approached the door, his flashlight revealing a control panel embedded in the wall. He glanced back at the group. "This is it. Ready?"

No one answered, but they all nodded, their faces mixed with fear and determination. Alex took a deep breath and reached for the panel, the soft hum of the Core growing louder as the door slid open.

The door groaned as it slid open, the grinding of metal against metal echoing ominously down the corridor. A blast of warm, stale air rushed out, carrying a faint hum that seemed to resonate in their chests. Beyond the threshold lay a massive chamber bathed in an eerie, pulsating blue light. The walls shimmered with strange, organic patterns like the room was alive.

The group hesitated at the entrance, their flashlights cutting through the dim glow. Alex took the first step inside, motioning for the others to follow. "Stay close. We don't know what's in here."

Erin lingered at the back, her glowing eyes wide as she stared at the Core—a towering structure of twisting, crystalline tendrils that pulsed rhythmically with energy. Sparks of blue light danced along its surface, shifting shadows across the chamber.

"That's it," Jamari whispered, his voice tinged with awe. "The Rift Nexus. The Core."

"Looks like something out of a sci-fi nightmare," Max muttered, gripping his flashlight tightly.

Sarah stepped closer to Erin, her voice gentle. "Are you okay?"

Erin didn't answer at first. Her eyes were fixed on the Core, her expression a mixture of fear and recognition. Finally, she whispered, "It's awake."

Before anyone could respond, a deep, guttural growl rumbled through the chamber, reverberating off the walls. The group spun around, their flashlights darting across the shadows. A shape began to emerge from the room's far end—tall, hunched, and bristling with unnatural energy. Its glowing eyes locked onto them, filled with primal, malevolent hunger.

"It's one of them," Logan said, raising his crowbar. "The shadow creatures."

"Everyone back!" Alex shouted, positioning himself between the group and the advancing creature.

The creature uttered a piercing shriek and charged, its elongated limbs moving with terrifying speed. Alex swung his crowbar, the impact sending a shower of sparks into the air, but the creature barely flinched. Sarah grabbed Erin, pulling her toward the far side of the chamber.

"Erin, can you do something?" Sarah pleaded.

Erin's hands trembled, her glowing eyes flickering brighter. "Too strong," she murmured. "But I... I can try."

Jamari frantically tapped at his PDA, searching for anything that might help. "The Core's energy is destabilizing. It might take the creature with it if we can overload it."

"Overload it?" Max shouted. "That'll take us out too!"

"We don't have a choice!" Jamari snapped.

Alex dodged another swipe from the creature, his movements growing slower as fatigue set in. "Jam, do it! We'll figure out the rest later."

Jamari nodded, his fingers flying across the PDA's screen. The chamber's hum grew louder, the light from the Core intensifying until it was almost blinding. The creature shrieked again, recoiling slightly as the energy surged around it.

Erin stepped forward, her hands raised. "Let me... help," she said, her voice steadier now. The glow in her eyes matched the Core's pulsating light as she reached out toward it. The tendrils of energy seemed to respond to her, bending and twisting toward her outstretched fingers.

"Erin, what are you doing?" Sarah shouted.

"Ending this," Erin replied.

The Core's light flared brighter than ever, filling the chamber with an overwhelming brilliance. The creature let out one final, agonized roar before its form disintegrated into a swirling vortex of shadows, sucked into the Core's energy.

The room shook violently, the walls cracking as the Core's pulsations grew erratic. Alex grabbed Erin, pulling her away from the tendrils as the structure collided. "We have to go! Now!"

The group sprinted back toward the hatch, dodging falling debris as the chamber crumbled around them. They scrambled up the ladder one by one, emerging into the ruins just as the ground beneath them gave way. Behind them, the Core erupted in a final burst of light and energy, the shockwave knocking them to the ground.

When the dust settled, the facility was silent once more, the hum of the Core replaced by an eerie stillness. Alex pushed himself to his feet, coughing as he looked around at his friends.

"Is everyone okay?" he asked.

"Define okay," Max muttered, wincing as he sat up.

Erin lay on the ground, her breathing shallow but steady. Sarah knelt beside her, relief flooding her face. "She's alive," she said softly. "She's okay."

Alex nodded, his gaze shifting to the smoldering ruins of Helix Labs. "We did it," he said, though his voice was heavy with exhaustion. "But this isn't over."

Jamari held up his PDA, the screen displaying fragments of data from the Core. "Whatever that thing was, it wasn't the only one. The Nexus might be gone, but the Rift... it's still open."

The group exchanged weary looks, the weight of their victory tempered by the knowledge of what still lay ahead. As they helped Erin to her feet and began the long trek back to Shadowridge, one thought echoed in their minds: the fight was far from finished.

The group arrived back at the barn under the cover of night, their bodies battered and their minds reeling from the events at Helix Labs.

The glow of the lantern inside felt like a beacon of safety as they filed in, one by one. Erin stumbled slightly, and Sarah caught her, guiding her to sit on the pile of blankets in the corner.

"We need to talk about what just happened," Alex said, leaning against the table as he caught his breath. "Erin, you connected to the Core. You did something to it. What was that?"

Erin's glowing eyes flickered as she stared at the floor, her hands trembling. "It... called to me," she said softly. "Familiar. Like... home, but wrong."

Sarah knelt beside her, speaking gently. "What do you mean? Was it something from before? From when you were at Helix Labs?"

Erin nodded slowly, her gaze distant. "They... made me. Tested me. Pain. Always pain."

The barn fell silent, the weight of her words settling over them. Jamari perched on a stool near the table, his PDA resting in his lap. "Do you remember what they were testing for?" he asked carefully.

Erin closed her eyes, her breathing uneven as fragmented memories surfaced. "Wanted... control. Power. Opened the Rift. Used us to... stabilize. But it didn't work. Broke things. Broke us."

Max shifted uncomfortably, running a hand through his hair. "You mean there were others? Like you?"

Her glowing eyes opened, filled with sorrow. "Yes. Many. Gone now. Lost."

"What happened to them?" Sarah asked, her voice barely above a whisper.

Erin's hands clenched into fists, her body trembling. "Some... couldn't handle it. Too much energy. Burned out. Others... changed. Became like... the shadow."

Alex exchanged a grim look with Logan. "The creatures we've been seeing. They were people?"

Erin nodded, tears streaming silently down her face. "They made them into monsters. I couldn't stop it. I... I tried. But they caught me. Locked me away."

Sarah wrapped an arm around Erin's shoulders, holding her close. "You're not there anymore. You're safe now."

"But for how long?" Logan asked, his voice laced with frustration. "The agents aren't going to stop. And if there are more creatures out there..."

"We have to figure out what's still connected to the Rift," Jamari said, his fingers tapping rapidly on his PDA. "If Helix Labs isn't the only site, there could be other places where they're continuing their work."

"You think it's still active?" Alex asked, crossing his arms.

"Maybe," Jamari replied. "Or maybe the Rift's instability is spreading. Either way, we're not done."

Erin's voice broke through the conversation, quiet but persistent. "I... remember something. A place. Another lab. Bigger. Deeper."

The group turned to her, their expressions a mix of dread and determination.

"Where?" Alex asked.

Erin hesitated, her glowing eyes narrowing as she pieced together the memory. "West. Mountains. Underground."

"Then that's where we're going next," Alex said, his tone leaving no room for argument. "If there's another lab, we'll find it and shut it down. For good."

The group nodded, their exhaustion momentarily forgotten in the face of their renewed mission. Erin looked around at her new friends, her expression softening despite the fear in her eyes. For the first time, she felt a glimmer of hope—a belief that she wasn't alone in this fight.

As the barn settled into a tense quiet, the faint sounds of the night outside seemed almost peaceful. But they all knew the peace wouldn't last. The battle was far from over, and their journey was beginning.

The barn was quiet as the group settled in for the night, their exhaustion palpable after the harrowing events at Helix Labs. Erin lay on the makeshift bed of blankets in the corner, breathing shallow as she drifted into an uneasy sleep. The others sat scattered around the room, speaking in hushed tones or staring into the lantern's dim glow.

But the peace didn't last.

Erin's screams tore through the stillness, raw and filled with pain. The group bolted upright, their hearts pounding as they rushed to her side. Erin thrashed wildly, her glowing eyes flaring with a brilliance that cast eerie shadows across the barn.

"Erin, wake up!" Sarah pleaded, kneeling beside her. She reached out to hold Erin's hand, but Erin pulled away, crying out as though reliving some unseen horror.

"It's okay! You're safe!" Alex said firmly, his voice steady despite the panic in his eyes.

Erin's breathing hitched, and her movements slowed as she blinked rapidly, her glowing eyes dimming. Tears streamed down her face as she sat up, clutching her knees.

"They hurt me," she whispered, her voice barely audible. "Again and again. I couldn't stop them. Couldn't... escape."

Sarah wrapped an arm around her, holding her close. "You're not there anymore. They can't hurt you now."

"But it's still inside me," Erin murmured, her voice trembling. "The pain. The... power. I don't know how to stop it."

The group exchanged uneasy glances. Jamari rubbed the back of his neck, his expression grim. "It might be the Core. You connected to it, Erin. Whatever it did... it might have left a mark."

"A mark?" Logan said, his tone sharp. "You mean like it changed her? Made her more unstable?"

"We don't know that," Sarah said defensively. "She's scared, and she needs us. That's what matters right now."

Erin's breathing began to even out, and her eyes slowly closed as she drifted back to sleep, exhaustion overtaking her once more. Sarah stayed by her side, stroking her hair gently. The others moved to the far side of the barn, their voices low but urgent.

"She's not okay," Logan said bluntly. "Whatever we did at Helix Labs... woke something up in her. And I don't think we can handle it."

"We don't have a choice," Alex said, his jaw tight. "She's one of us now. We're not abandoning her."

"I'm not saying we should," Logan shot back. "But we need to be realistic. If this gets worse, what happens to her? To us?"

Max sighed, leaning against the wall. "Look, I'm freaked out too, okay? But she's not a monster. She's scared and confused, just like we'd be if we went through what she did."

"And if the agents come after her again?" Jamari asked, his voice tight. "What if they find us? Or worse, what if she can't control her powers next time?"

Alex's gaze shifted to Erin, her small frame curled up on the blankets as Sarah watched over her. His expression softened. "Then we help her. We figure out how to get her through this, no matter what it takes."

"And if we can't?" Logan pressed.

"We will," Alex said firmly. "Because we're all she's got."

The group fell silent, the weight of Alex's words settling over them. Outside, the wind rustled the trees, a quiet reminder of the dangers lurking beyond their fragile sanctuary. For now, all they could do was wait and hope that morning would bring some semblance of clarity—and that Erin's nightmares wouldn't become their reality.

As the first light of dawn crept through the cracks in the barn walls, the group stirred from their uneasy rest. Erin sat by the window, her glowing eyes fixed on the horizon, where the sun cast long shadows across the trees. She looked tired but calmer, her hands steady as she held a mug of water Sarah had given her.

Alex approached quietly, sitting beside her. "How are you holding up?" he asked.

Erin didn't look at him right away, her gaze distant. "It's quieter now," she said softly. "But it's still there. Always there."

"We'll figure it out," Alex said firmly. "You're not alone in this."

Erin finally turned to him, her expression a mix of gratitude and fear. "Thank you," she whispered.

The rest of the group gathered slowly, faces lined with exhaustion but clear resolve. Jamari adjusted his PDA, which now displayed a rough region map. "I found something based on what Erin said about the other lab. There's an old military installation in the foothills west of here. It's been decommissioned for years, but if Helix Labs was using it…"

"Then that's where we're going next," Alex finished, standing. "Whatever's out there, it's the key to ending this."

Sarah glanced at Erin, her brow furrowed with concern. "But is she ready for this? We saw what connecting to the Core did to her. What if it's too much?"

Erin stood slowly, her glowing eyes meeting Sarah's. "I have to try. If I don't… more will suffer. More will die."

Logan leaned against the wall, crossing his arms. "She's tougher than she looks," he said grudgingly. "But we need to be ready for whatever's out there. No more surprises."

Max let out a nervous laugh. "Yeah, because we've been great at avoiding those."

Despite the tension, a faint smile crossed Erin's face. For the first time, she felt something other than fear in their presence—she felt trust.

Alex looked at each of them in turn, his voice steady. "This is bigger than any of us, but we're together. We've made it this far, and we're not giving up now."

The group nodded, their determination solidifying as they began packing their gear. The barn, which had served as their refuge, now felt like a launching point for something greater. As they stepped out into the morning light, the horizon ahead seemed daunting and full of promise.

But as they set off toward the mountains, they carried with them the hope that they could rewrite the story Helix Labs had tried to script together.

Chapter 6: Into the Mountains

The wind picked up as the group left Shadowridge behind, their bikes cutting through the quiet morning streets. Each carried a small pack filled with supplies—flashlights, food, and whatever tools they could gather from their homes. Erin sat quietly in the wagon attached to Jamari's bike, her glowing eyes scanning the horizon as they pedaled toward the western foothills.

"Are we sure about this?" Max asked, breaking the silence. He swerved slightly to avoid a pothole, his voice tight with nerves. "This isn't exactly a quick trip to the arcade."

"It's the only lead we have," Alex replied, his voice steady. He pedaled ahead of the group, his gaze fixed on the winding road that disappeared into the distant trees. "If Helix Labs is using that installation, we must find out what they're doing."

"And shut it down," Logan added, gripping his handlebars tightly. "Before they make more of those creatures."

Sarah glanced back at Erin, who sat with her knees drawn to her chest. "How are you holding up?" she asked softly.

Erin hesitated before answering, her voice barely above a whisper. "Afraid... but ready. Have to be."

The group exchanged uneasy looks, but no one said anything. The truth was, they were all afraid. The events at Helix Labs had shaken them, and the uncertainty of what lay ahead was a heavy weight on their shoulders.

The journey to the installation was simple. The group had chosen backroads and overgrown trails to avoid attention, winding through Shadowridge's outskirts and into increasingly dense woodland. The air felt heavier the further they traveled, as if the forest carried the weight of their mission.

"How much farther?" Max asked, his voice breaking the quiet. He pedaled hard, sweat forming on his brow despite the cool air. "Feels like we've been going for hours."

Jamari pulled out his PDA, its dim screen glowing faintly in the growing shadows. "We're about halfway there," he said, squinting at the map. "But these paths aren't exactly made for bikes. We might need to walk the rest of the way."

"Great," Max muttered. "Because lugging all this gear isn't enough fun already."

Alex glanced back at Erin, who sat quietly in the wagon. She hadn't spoken much since they left, her glowing eyes darting nervously between the trees. "You doing okay back there?" he asked.

Erin's gaze met his briefly before returning to the forest. "Quiet here," she said softly. "But... not safe."

The group fell silent at her words, their unease growing as they pushed on. The path narrowed, forcing them to dismount and walk their bikes through thick underbrush. The forest seemed darker now, the canopy above blotting out the sun.

"This place gives me the creeps," Logan said, his voice low. He carried his crowbar like a talisman, his eyes scanning the shadows. "Feels like we're being watched."

"We probably are," Sarah said, her tone matter-of-fact. "If Helix Labs has patrols or sensors, they'd be all over a place like this."

"Sensors?" Max said, his voice rising. "And you're telling me this now?"

"Relax," Jamari said, holding up his PDA. "I've been scanning for signals. Nothing's pinged so far. That doesn't mean we're in the clear, though."

As they reached a small clearing, Alex called for a break. The group collapsed onto the soft grass, grateful for the momentary reprieve. Erin sat apart from the others, her knees drawn to her chest as she stared into the distance.

Sarah joined her, sitting cross-legged nearby. "What's on your mind?" she asked gently.

Erin's glowing eyes flickered. "Feels... close like before. I can't explain. ... feels wrong."

Sarah frowned, glancing back at Alex. "She thinks we're near something."

"That's comforting," Logan said dryly, taking a swig from his water bottle.

"We'll stay sharp," Alex said, standing. "Let's keep moving. We need to reach the site before dark."

The final stretch of their journey was the hardest. The terrain grew steeper, and the dense forest gave way to jagged rocks and loose gravel. Their bikes became burdens, forcing them to carry them over rough patches of trail. The occasional sound of wildlife only heightened their anxiety, every rustle of leaves or snap of a twig sending their nerves into overdrive.

By the time they crested the ridge, the sun had dipped low in the sky, casting a fiery glow over the landscape. Below them, the installation came into view. From this height, the compound looked deceptively peaceful, its low buildings blending into the surrounding forest. But even from a distance, the faint plumes of smoke rising from one of the chimneys hinted at activity within.

The group paused, taking in the sight. Max let out a low whistle. "Well, there it is. Creepy enough for everyone?"

"Still active," Jamari said, adjusting his binoculars. "Can't see any patrols, but that doesn't mean they're not there."

Alex crouched, motioning for the others to do the same. "We wait until nightfall," he said. "Get some rest while you can. Once it's dark, we move in."

The group exchanged tense nods, each acutely aware of the risks ahead as they settled into the underbrush. The forest around them seemed to grow quieter, and the anticipation of their mission was hanging heavy in the air.

The road grew steeper as they reached the edge of the foothills. Towering trees lined the path, their branches forming a canopy that filtered the sunlight into shifting patterns on the ground. The air was cooler here, carrying the faint scent of pine and damp earth.

Jamari slowed his bike, pulling up alongside Alex. "We're getting close," he said, checking the map on his PDA. "The installation should be just over that ridge."

"What's the plan when we get there?" Max asked, his voice edged with tension. "Because I'm not thrilled about walking into another monster nest."

"We scout first," Alex said. "Find a way in and figure out what we're dealing with. No unnecessary risks."

"That's optimistic," Logan muttered.

"We'll be careful," Sarah said firmly, cutting off the brewing argument. She glanced at Erin, who was watching the trees with a distant expression. "Right, Erin?"

Erin nodded, though her gaze remained unfocused. "Quiet. Careful. Like shadows."

They reached the top of the ridge as the sun dipped lower in the sky, casting long shadows over the forest. From their vantage point, they could see the installation—a cluster of low, squat buildings partially hidden by the dense trees. A chain-link fence surrounded the perimeter, topped with rusted barbed wire. The structures looked abandoned at first glance, but faint plumes of smoke rising from one of the chimneys suggested otherwise.

"So much for decommissioned," Jamari muttered, zooming in on the site with the small binoculars he'd brought. "Looks like someone's still home."

"Agents?" Logan asked.

"Maybe," Jamari replied. "Or worse."

Alex crouched beside him, his expression grim. "We'll wait until nightfall. Better cover that way."

The group settled into the underbrush, their nerves on edge as they watched the installation from afar. As the hours passed, the forest came alive with the sounds of nocturnal creatures. The sky darkened, and the first stars appeared overhead, their faint light doing little to ease the tension.

"How do we know it's not a trap?" Max whispered, his voice barely audible.

"We don't," Alex admitted. "But we're here now. We'll stick to the plan."

Erin's voice broke through the hushed conversation, soft but steady. "It's not a trap. It's... something else. They're waiting."

Sarah frowned, leaning closer to her. "Waiting for what?"

Erin's glowing eyes flickered, her expression distant. "For us."

The group huddled in the underbrush as the last light of day faded, leaving the forest cloaked in shadow. Above them, the first stars began to dot the sky, their faint glow offering little comfort. Jamari adjusted the binoculars, scanning the installation below for any signs of movement.

"Still nothing," he whispered, lowering the lenses. "If there are guards, they're either inside or good at hiding."

"Let's assume both," Alex said. He crouched beside Jamari, his voice low but firm. "We stick to the plan. Jam and I will scout ahead. The rest of you wait here until we give the signal."

Sarah frowned, glancing at Erin. "What about her? She shouldn't be left alone."

"I'll stay with her," Logan volunteered, gripping his crowbar. "And Max, because someone has to keep him quiet."

"Funny," Max muttered, rolling his eyes but giving a faint grin.

Erin's glowing eyes flickered in the darkness. "Be careful," she said softly, her voice tinged with worry.

Alex gave her a reassuring nod before turning to Jamari. "Let's move."

The two crept down the ridge, their movements careful and deliberate. As they approached the installation, the forest thinned, the ground transitioning to gravel and packed dirt. The air grew colder, and the faint hum of machinery became audible, cutting through the stillness.

They reached the perimeter fence and crouched low, scanning for an opening. Jamari's PDA emitted a faint beep, and the screen displayed a grid-like overlay of the site.

"Looks like the main building has multiple entry points," he whispered. "But the north side is closest to the lab Erin mentioned."

Alex nodded, his eyes narrowing as he spotted a section of the fence where the barbed wire had rusted away. "There. We can get through."

They moved quickly, slipping through the gap and into the compound. The buildings loomed around them, their facades cracked and weathered but still imposing. A single light flickered above the north entrance, casting long shadows across the concrete.

Jamari paused, his PDA beeping softly. "Motion sensor ahead," he said, pointing to a small device near the door.

Alex frowned. "Can you disable it?"

"Give me a minute," Jamari replied, pulling a small toolkit from his bag. He knelt by the device, his fingers deftly working to override the circuitry. After a tense moment, the light on the sensor blinked off.

"Done," he whispered, stepping back.

Alex tested the door, finding it unlocked. He pushed it open cautiously, revealing a narrow hallway lined with flickering fluorescent lights. The hum of machinery grew louder, accompanied by the faint hiss of steam.

"We're in," Alex said into his walkie-talkie. "Bring the others."

Back at the ridge, Logan, Sarah, Max, and Erin waited anxiously. The walkie-talkie crackled, and Alex's voice came through. "We're clear. Move now."

"Finally," Max muttered, grabbing his backpack. "Sitting around was starting to drive me crazy."

"Everything drives you crazy," Logan said, smirking as he helped Erin.

The group went down the ridge, moving as quietly as possible. Erin clung to Sarah, her glowing eyes darting nervously toward every sound. When they reached the fence, Logan helped her through the gap, his grip firm but gentle.

They followed Alex's directions inside the compound, weaving through the shadows until they reached the north entrance. Alex and Jamari were waiting, their expressions tense.

"No guards yet," Alex said, "but that doesn't mean we're alone."

Erin stepped forward, her gaze fixed on the hallway ahead. "It's here," she said softly. "The lab. The place they took us."

"Then let's finish this," Alex said, motioning for the group to follow.

The hallway led to a heavy steel door marked with faded warnings and the Helix Labs logo. Jamari examined the control panel beside it, frowning as he tapped at the screen.

"This is more advanced than the last place," he said. "I'll need a few minutes."

"We might not have that," Logan said, eyes scanning the hallway. "Hurry it up."

As Jamari worked, Erin stepped closer to the door, her hands trembling. She placed a palm against the cold metal, her glowing eyes flaring briefly.

"What is it?" Sarah asked, her voice gentle.

Erin's expression was distant, her voice barely a whisper. "Memories. Pain. It's all still here."

Alex placed a hand on her shoulder, his tone firm but reassuring. "We're here to stop it. Whatever they did to you, we'll ensure it ends here."

The panel beeped, and the door slid open with a hiss. Beyond it was a massive chamber filled with rows of glass tanks, their contents obscured by a thick, greenish mist. The hum of machinery was deafening now, and the air felt charged with an unnatural energy.

"What the hell is this place?" Max whispered, his voice trembling.

"A factory," Jamari said grimly. "They're still making them."

"The creatures," Logan said, gripping his crowbar tighter. "This is where they're coming from."

Erin stepped forward, her glowing eyes fixed on the tanks. "Not just them," she said. "There's something worse. Deeper."

Alex exchanged a tense glance with the group. "Then we keep moving. Whatever's down there, we're shutting it down for good."

The group stepped cautiously into the chamber, their footsteps muffled by the hum of machinery and the faint hiss of steam escaping from pipes. The mist hung thick in the air, its greenish hue giving the room an otherworldly quality. Rows of glass tanks lined the walls, each connected to a network of tubes and wires that disappeared into the floor.

Max peered into one of the tanks, wiping away condensation with his sleeve. His face paled as he took in the sight of what lay inside. "Oh, no. No, no, no..."

"What is it?" Sarah asked, moving to stand beside him. Her gasp echoed in the chamber as she saw the distorted figure floating in the viscous liquid. It was humanoid, but its features were wrong—elongated limbs, sharp claws, and eyes that glowed faintly even through the fluid.

"They're not just making more creatures," Jamari said, his voice tight as he examined the tanks. "They're experimenting with them. Modifying them."

Erin stood frozen, her glowing eyes wide as she stared at the rows of tanks. "This is... where they took us. Where they made us."

Alex approached one of the tanks, his jaw tightening as he studied the figure inside. "They're still running the program. Whatever they started with the Rift, they're still trying to perfect it."

"Perfect it for what?" Logan asked, his voice low but filled with anger. "What could anyone possibly need this for?"

"Weapons," Erin said, her voice barely a whisper. "That's what we were supposed to be. Weapons for them to use. But it... got out of control."

The group exchanged uneasy glances, the weight of Erin's words settling over them like a heavy fog. Alex turned to Jamari, his expression resolute. "We need to find the control center. If we can shut this place down, we might be able to stop this for good."

Jamari nodded, pulling up the schematics on his PDA. "The control room should be at the far end of the chamber. But it's not going to be unguarded."

A low growl echoed through the chamber as if on cue, reverberating off the metal walls. The group froze, their flashlights darting across the shadows. From the far side of the room, a figure emerged—tall, hunched, and bristling with the same unnatural energy as the creatures they'd faced before.

"Of course," Max muttered, gripping a length of pipe he'd picked up earlier. "Because it wasn't creepy enough already."

Alex raised his crowbar, his voice steady despite the fear in his eyes. "Get to the control room. I'll hold it off."

"You can't fight that thing alone," Sarah protested, stepping beside him.

"I won't be alone," Alex said, glancing at Logan, who nodded grimly and stepped forward.

"We'll buy you time," Logan said, his knuckles white as he gripped his weapon. "Go."

Sarah hesitated, torn, but Jamari tugged at her arm. "Come on. We have to move."

With Erin in tow, the rest of the group sprinted toward the chamber's far end, weaving between the rows of tanks. The creature's snarls echoed behind them, and metal clashed against claws.

They reached the control center, a small room enclosed by glass walls. Jamari immediately set to work on the console, his fingers flying across the keyboard. The screens flickered to life, displaying data streams and camera feeds across the facility.

"Can you shut it down?" Sarah asked, her voice urgent.

"I'm trying," Jamari replied, sweat beading his forehead. "But it's not just a switch I can flip. This system is locked down tight."

Erin stepped forward, her glowing eyes narrowing as she stared at the console. "I can help," she said, her voice steady despite the fear in her expression.

Jamari hesitated. "Are you sure? Last time you connected to something like this, it almost—"

"I have to," Erin interrupted, touching the console. The screens flickered wildly as her energy surged through the system, and the machinery's hum grew louder.

Sarah placed a reassuring hand on Erin's shoulder. "We're here. You've got this."

The chamber shook as the system began to overload, sparks flying from the equipment. The tanks lining the walls cracked under the strain, their contents sloshing against the glass. Erin winced, her breathing labored, but she didn't let go.

"Almost there," Jamari said, his eyes darting between the monitors. "Just a little longer."

The creature's roar echoed through the chamber, louder and closer than before. Sarah turned toward the door, her heart pounding. "We're out of time."

Erin's eyes flared brightly, and the system whined loudly. With a final surge of energy, the entire facility went dark, the hum of machinery replaced by an eerie silence. The tanks shattered one by one, their contents spilling onto the floor.

Alex and Logan appeared in the doorway, their faces bruised and bloodied but alive. "Time to go!" Alex shouted.

As they moved through the control room, Sarah paused, her gaze falling on a stack of folders scattered across a nearby desk. "Wait," she said, grabbing them quickly. "These might tell us more about what they were doing here." The others hesitated for only a moment before agreeing to press on.

The group sprinted back through the chamber, dodging the collapsing infrastructure and the writhing remains of failed experiments. Along the way, their flashlights illuminated eerie remnants—scrawled notes pinned to walls in handwriting that grew increasingly erratic, strange metallic artifacts pulsing faintly with energy, and cryptic diagrams of what appeared to be portals or dimensional rifts. The air grew thick with smoke and the acrid smell of burning machinery as the facility self-destructed.

They emerged into the cool night air, coughing and gasping for breath. Behind them, the installation erupted in a final, blinding explosion, sending a shockwave that knocked them to the ground.

For a moment, there was only silence. Then Alex pushed himself up, coughing as he looked around at his friends. "Is everyone okay?"

"Define okay," Max said weakly, sitting up and rubbing his head.

Erin lay on the ground, her glowing eyes dim but still alight. Sarah knelt beside her, brushing a strand of hair from her face. "You did it," Sarah said softly. "You stopped it."

Erin nodded faintly, a small, tired smile crossing her face. "Not over," she murmured. "Just... beginning."

The group exchanged uneasy glances, the weight of her words settling over them as they helped each other to their feet. The facility was gone, but the fight was far from finished. Together, they turned and began the long journey back to Shadowridge, their bonds more potent than ever and their resolve unshaken.

The journey back to Shadowridge was silent; each group member was lost in their thoughts. Erin sat in the wagon, her glowing eyes dim as she clutched the folder Sarah had grabbed from the control room. The faint light of dawn began to creep over the horizon as they neared the outskirts of town, painting the empty streets in hues of orange and pink.

Exhaustion had set in when they reached the barn, but no one suggested resting. Alex propped his bike against the wall, turning to the others. "Let's see what we're dealing with," he said, motioning to the folder in Erin's hands.

Inside, Sarah spread the files out on the table, careful not to smudge the faded ink or tear the brittle pages. Jamari leaned over them, his PDA ready to scan anything requiring decoding.

"These look old," Sarah said, her voice low. "Like they've been here since the beginning of the project."

Jamari picked up one of the documents, his brow furrowing as he scanned the handwritten notes. "These are lab reports," he said. "Mostly observations on... whatever they were creating. Numbers, not names, identify subjects. It's all very clinical."

"What does it say about Erin?" Sarah asked, glancing at the girl, who sat quietly on a pile of blankets.

Jamari flipped through the pages until he found one marked "MW3746"—Erin's designation. His face grew pale as he read aloud. "'Subject demonstrates unique resonance with Rift energy. Potential to stabilize or amplify dimensional gateways. High risk of overload.'" He paused, swallowing hard. "'Recommended for isolation and direct experimentation with Core fragments.'"

Erin flinched at the words, her hands trembling. "They... wanted to use me," she said softly. "To make the Rift stronger."

Alex's fists clenched, anger flashing in his eyes. "They didn't care what it did to you," he said. "You were just a tool to them."

"What else is there?" Logan asked, his voice tense.

Jamari flipped to another page, his brow furrowing deeper. "There's mention of 'The Beacon,' something they were building to anchor the Rift... permanently. If this was just a test site, the main Beacon could still be active there."

"Where?" Max asked, leaning in.

"It doesn't say," Jamari replied, frustration creeping into his voice. "But there are coordinates here. They might point to another site."

"Another lab?" Sarah said, her expression grim.

"Or worse," Jamari replied. "If the Beacon is operational, it's not just creating creatures. It's ripping the Rift open wider. That could explain why the energy feels stronger... and the creatures are getting more aggressive."

Erin's voice broke through the tense silence. "We have to stop it," she said, her glowing eyes meeting Alex's. "Before it's too late."

Alex nodded, his resolve firm. "Then we follow the coordinates. Whatever's out there, we'll find it and shut it down."

Jamari began scanning the documents into his PDA, his fingers moving quickly over the screen. "Give me a little time to cross-reference these with the data we've already collected. If there's a pattern, I'll find it."

"Good," Alex said. He turned to the rest of the group. "Get some rest while you can. Once we have a lead, we're moving out."

The group nodded, each retreating to its corner of the barn. As the others tried to find some semblance of rest, Jamari stayed at the table, the soft glow of his PDA illuminating his determined expression. The weight of their discovery hung heavy in the air, but beneath it was a shared resolve: they would stop Helix Labs and the Beacon, no matter the cost.

The barn settled into an uneasy quiet as the morning sun climbed higher in the sky. Erin sat by the window, her glowing eyes dim but watchful. Sarah joined her, offering a faint smile as she placed a hand on her shoulder.

"You did good back there," Sarah said softly. "I know it's a lot, but you're stronger than you think."

Erin's gaze flickered to Sarah, a small, grateful smile breaking through her tired expression. "I'm not strong," she said. "Not like you."

"We're all strong in our way," Sarah replied. "And together? We're unstoppable."

Across the room, Jamari leaned back from the table, rubbing his eyes as his PDA chirped faintly. "Got something," he said, his voice tinged with exhaustion and excitement. "The coordinates point to a location further west—way out in the middle of nowhere. Looks like an old mining site."

"Makes sense," Logan said, joining him at the table. "A remote location would be perfect if they hide something big."

"Big doesn't even begin to cover it," Jamari said, tapping the screen. "From how these files describe it, this Beacon is designed to hold the Rift open indefinitely. If it's already active..."

"Then we're out of time," Alex said, his voice firm. He stood, his gaze sweeping over the group. "We leave tonight. Get some rest, double-check your gear, and be ready. This is going to be the hardest thing we've faced yet."

Max groaned but nodded, flopping onto a pile of hay. "Great. There is more running, more monsters, and probably more almost dying. Can't wait."

Despite the tension, a faint chuckle rippled through the group, lightening the mood just enough to make the task ahead seem possible.

Erin stood, her glowing eyes brighter now. "I'm ready," she said, her voice steady. "Whatever happens, I won't let them win."

Alex gave her a nod; his respect was evident. "None of us will."

As the group began to prepare for their next mission, the air in the barn shifted. Fear and uncertainty were still present, but so was something more substantial: determination. Together, they were ready to face whatever awaited them at the Beacon.

Chapter 7: The Shadow Entity

The forest near the Beacon site was eerily quiet as the group pushed through the thick underbrush. They were close now, each step bringing them nearer to the remote mining facility identified in the files. The air felt heavier here, oppressive and charged with an unnatural energy that made the hairs on their necks stand on end.

"I don't like this," Max whispered, his voice trembling as he adjusted the beam of his flashlight. "It's too quiet."

"You think?" Logan muttered, gripping his crowbar tighter. His eyes scanned the surrounding trees, his posture tense. "Feels like something's watching us."

"It is," Erin said suddenly, her glowing eyes narrowing as she came to a halt. The group froze, their breath catching in their throats.

"What do you mean, 'it is'?" Sarah asked, her voice barely above a whisper.

Erin pointed into the darkness, her hand trembling. "It's here. Watching. Waiting."

Before anyone could respond, a low, guttural growl rumbled through the trees, sending a shiver down their spines. The sound was unnatural, a mixture of a feral snarl and something far more sinister. The group huddled together, their flashlights darting across the shadows.

"Stay close," Alex ordered, his voice steady despite the fear gnawing at him. "And keep moving. Whatever it is, we can't let it pin us down."

They pressed on, the growls growing louder and more frequent, echoing from all directions. The proximity to the Beacon's suspected location only heightened their unease. The forest seemed to close around them, the twisted branches above blocking the moonlight as if nature conspired to trap them. Max tripped over a root, letting out a yelp that Logan quickly muffled.

"Shh," Logan hissed. "Do you want to bring it right to us?"

"I think it already knows where we are," Jamari said, his voice tight. He held up his PDA, which was emitting a faint, erratic beeping. "This thing is going haywire. Whatever's out there, it's putting off some serious energy."

A sudden rustling to their left made them all spin around, their flashlights converging on the source. The light illuminated only trees and undergrowth, yet the oppressive feeling grew more assertive.

"It's playing with us," Erin said, trembling but resolute. "Testing us."

"Well, I'm not a fan of pop quizzes," Max muttered.

Before anyone could respond, a massive shadow burst from the trees, its form shifting and writhing as though it were made of living darkness. Glowing red eyes pierced through the black mass, locking onto Erin. The creature let out an ear-splitting roar, and the group scattered instinctively.

"Run!" Alex shouted, grabbing Erin's arm and pulling her with him as the others sprinted in different directions.

They sprinted through the tangled underbrush, the oppressive atmosphere of the forest pressing down on them with every step. Erin's legs faltered, her breath coming in shallow gasps, but Sarah was at her side instantly, pulling her forward.

"You're okay," Sarah whispered urgently. "Just a little further."

The growls behind them grew louder, echoing like a sinister chorus through the trees. Alex glanced back, his flashlight catching a fleeting glimpse of the shadowy entity—its shifting form melting into the darkness as it pursued them.

"This thing isn't letting up," Logan said through gritted teeth, gripping his crowbar like a lifeline. "Where's the clearing, Jamari?"

Jamari checked his PDA, and the screen was flickering with interference. "Just ahead," he called, pointing through the trees. "We'll be more exposed there, but it's better than getting cornered here."

"Then keep moving," Alex ordered.

They broke into a final sprint, bursting through the dense underbrush and into a small clearing illuminated faintly by the sliver of moonlight that managed to break through the canopy. Their breaths came in ragged gasps as they regrouped, forming a defensive circle with Erin in the center.

The group regrouped in a small clearing, their breaths coming in ragged gasps. The creature didn't follow immediately, but its guttural growls echoed in the distance, a reminder that it was still hunting them.

"What the hell was that thing?" Logan demanded, his crowbar raised defensively as he scanned the treeline.

"I don't know," Alex admitted, his voice tight. "But it's after Erin."

Erin stepped forward, her glowing eyes brighter now, filled with fear and determination. "It's not just after me," she said. "It's connected to me. I can feel it."

Before anyone could process her words, the creature burst into the clearing, its massive form towering over them. Alex and Logan moved to the front, raising their weapons, but Erin stepped between them, her hands glowing with an intense blue light.

"Erin, what are you doing?" Sarah shouted.

"Stopping it," Erin replied.

With a burst of energy, she thrust her hands forward, releasing a wave of light that collided with the shadow creature. The impact sent the beast reeling, its form flickering and distorting as if struggling to maintain cohesion. The clearing was bathed in an ethereal glow, the power emanating from Erin almost blinding.

But the effort took its toll. Erin collapsed to the ground, unconscious, as the light faded. The creature let out a final, enraged roar before retreating into the darkness.

"Erin!" Sarah cried, rushing to her side. She shook her gently, but Erin didn't respond.

"Is she okay?" Jamari asked, kneeling beside her.

"She's breathing," Sarah said, relief washing over her. "But we need to get her somewhere safe."

They carried Erin through the forest, eventually stumbling upon a small, rundown cabin among the trees. The place was cluttered with papers, strange contraptions, and shelves lined with jars of unidentifiable substances. A man emerged from the shadows, his eyes wide with curiosity and recognition as they entered.

"Well, well," he said, his voice gravelly but tinged with excitement. "Didn't expect to see MW3746 out here."

The group froze, their exhaustion momentarily forgotten.

"Who are you?" Alex demanded, stepping protectively in front of Erin.

The man smirked, adjusting his tattered coat. "Name's Elias. Most folks around here call me crazy, but I've seen things. Things people wouldn't believe. And I know what she is." He pointed to Erin.

"How do you know about her?" Sarah asked, her voice wary.

Elias chuckled, moving to a cluttered desk and pulling out a faded file. "Because I've been tracking Helix Labs for years. And she's one of their biggest secrets."

He looked at Erin with a mix of wonder and sadness. "But seeing her like this? I didn't think any of you were still... functional."

The group exchanged uneasy glances as Erin stirred faintly, her glowing eyes opening just enough to lock onto Elias. "I... know you," she whispered before slipping back unconscious.

Elias's expression darkened. "Then we've got a lot to talk about."

Alex and Logan lowered Erin onto the couch, her breathing still shallow but steady. The group gathered around, their nerves on edge as Elias sat at a cluttered table, rummaging through a pile of papers.

"She's one of their experiments," Elias began, his tone matter-of-fact. "They made her interact with the Rift. A conduit, you might say, to channel its energy. But they didn't count on the side effects."

"Side effects?" Jamari prompted, his PDA poised to record.

Elias nodded grimly. "Like that connection, she has with the shadow thing. That's no coincidence. The Rift... it's alive in some way. Sentient, even. And she's tied to it more closely than anyone they've made before."

Sarah's eyes widened. "So the shadow entity... it's part of the Rift?"

"Or it's what's guarding it," Elias said. "Either way, it sees her as part of itself. That's why it's hunting her. It's not just after her... it wants her back."

A heavy silence filled the room as the group processed Elias's words. Alex crossed his arms, his expression hardening. "Well, it's not getting her. Whatever Helix Labs started, we're going to end it."

Elias chuckled, shaking his head. "You've got guts, kid. But you will need more than bravery if you want to stop this. You'll need to understand what you're up against. And for that, you're going to need my help."

Alex hesitated, glancing at the others. Finally, he nodded. "Alright, Elias. Start talking."

Elias gestured toward a worn-out couch. "Lay her down there," he said. "And I'll tell you what I know."

Erin stirred on the couch, her glowing eyes flickering as she came to. The room was dim, lit only by a flickering oil lamp on Elias's cluttered desk. She bolted upright, her breaths coming in rapid gasps as her gaze locked onto the unfamiliar surroundings and then onto Elias.

"No," she whispered, her voice trembling. She scrambled back, pressing herself against the armrest as if trying to disappear. "Not again. Not them."

"Hey, hey, it's okay," Sarah said quickly, moving to her side and gently taking her hands. "You're safe. He's not one of them."

Elias held up his hands, keeping his distance. "Easy there, kid. I'm not with Helix Labs. If I were, I wouldn't be here helping your friends keep you out of their clutches."

Erin's glowing eyes darted between Sarah and Elias, her fear palpable. "Who is he?" she asked, her voice barely audible.

"His name's Elias," Alex said, stepping closer but keeping his tone calm. "He knows about Helix Labs and the Rift. He knows about you, too."

Erin's gaze narrowed. "How?"

Elias leaned against the edge of his desk, his expression softening. "Because I've been watching them for years," he said. "I've seen what they do. How they take people... kids like you... and twist them into something they can use. But you? You're different. Special. They gave you a designation: MW3746. But you're not just a number to them. You're their masterpiece."

Erin shivered, her hands clutching the blanket Sarah had draped over her. "I don't want to be there anything," she said, her voice shaking. "I didn't ask for this."

"I know," Elias said, his tone gentle. "And that's why I'm here. To help you fight back. To help all of you fight back."

Sarah sat beside Erin, her arm around her shoulders. "You said you know what she is. What does that mean?"

Elias sighed, running a hand through his wild hair. "It means Helix Labs didn't just give her powers. They made her a part of the Rift itself. She can sense it, interact with it, and... well, you saw what she did back there. That power? It's not just from her. It's from the Rift. That's why the shadow entity is after her. To the Rift, she's like a piece of itself walking around the world."

Erin stared at him, her expression a mix of fear and disbelief. "I'm... part of it?"

Elias nodded. "In a way, yeah. But that doesn't mean you belong to it. You've got a choice, kid. You can let it control you, or you can fight it. And with your friends here, you've got a pretty good shot at winning."

The room fell quiet after Elias's explanation, the only sound the faint creak of the cabin settling in the night. Erin sat motionless, her glowing eyes fixed on the flickering lamp. Her mind raced with the weight of Elias's words—that she wasn't just connected to the Rift but a part of it.

"I still don't understand," she finally said, trembling. "If I'm part of the Rift, why didn't it just take me back when it had the chance?"

Elias leaned forward, his sharp gaze meeting hers. "Because you're not just a part of it—you're something more. You have the power to channel its energy and the will to resist it. That makes you dangerous to the Rift and to Helix Labs."

"Dangerous, how?" Alex asked, crossing his arms. "What can she do that they're so afraid of?"

Elias gestured toward Erin. "If she learns to control her connection, she could close the Rift. Permanently. That would end their experiments, destroy the Beacon, and cut off whatever they're trying to bring through. But it's not without risks. The Rift might not let go so easily."

The group exchanged uneasy glances. Sarah placed a hand on Erin's shoulder. "You don't have to do this alone," she said softly. "We'll figure it out together."

Erin nodded slowly, her expression resolute despite the fear in her eyes. "What do we do next?"

Elias stood, rummaging through a pile of papers and maps on his desk. "We start by finding the Beacon. If Helix Labs has activated it, the energy signature will be massive. It's probably why the shadow entity is getting more aggressive—it's being drawn to the Beacon, just like Erin."

Jamari pulled out his PDA, syncing it with one of the old maps Elias handed him. "These coordinates match what we found in the lab," he said. "Looks like the Beacon is deep in the mountains, near an old mining site. If it's operational, we'll need to move fast."

"Fast is one thing," Logan said, leaning against the wall. "But we need a plan. We might not get lucky twice if that thing comes after us again."

Elias nodded. "Agreed. The shadow entity won't stop until it gets what it wants. But now that Erin's power has surfaced, we might be able to use it against it. You need training."

"Training?" Max exclaimed, incredulous. "You make it sound like she's signing up for superhero boot camp."

"More like survival training," Elias said, unfazed. "The Rift's energy is unpredictable, but with focus, Erin can learn to control it. And we'll need that edge if we take down the Beacon."

Alex turned to Erin, his expression firm. "What do you think? Are you up for this?"

Erin hesitated, then nodded. "If it means stopping Helix Labs and the Rift... I'll do whatever it takes."

Elias smiled faintly. "Good. Then, let's get started. We don't have much time."

As the group prepared for the journey, Elias began outlining the basics of channeling energy. Using old diagrams and cryptic notes from Helix Labs, he explained how Erin's connection to the Rift could be both a weapon and a shield.

"It's like a storm," Elias said, pacing the cabin. "Unpredictable and destructive if left unchecked. But if you focus, you can direct it. Use it. The trick is not letting it overwhelm you."

Erin stood in the center of the room, her hands trembling as she tried to summon the glowing energy she had felt before. The others watched anxiously, their faces a mix of awe and concern.

"You've got this," Sarah encouraged. "Just breathe and take it slow."

Erin closed her eyes, focusing on the faint hum of power she could feel deep within her. A soft blue glow slowly emanated from her hands, illuminating the room. The light flickered at first but grew stronger as she concentrated.

"Good," Elias said, his voice calm but firm. "Now, hold it. Don't let it slip away."

A sudden crackle of energy jolted through the room, and Erin gasped. The glow disappeared as she staggered back. Sarah caught her before she fell, and the group rushed to her side.

"I'm okay," Erin said, her breathing ragged. "It's just... harder than I thought."

"That's normal," Elias reassured her. "It'll take time, but you're already stronger than you know."

The group exchanged determined looks, the gravity of their mission settling over them once more. They were heading into the unknown, but for the first time, they felt like they had a chance.

As the first light of dawn crept through the cracks in the cabin walls, Elias spread a map across the table. "This is it," he said, pointing to a remote location deep in the mountains. "The Beacon is here. If we're lucky, we can shut it down before Helix Labs sends reinforcements."

"Lucky isn't exactly our strong suit," Max muttered, earning a small smile from the group.

Alex straightened, his voice unwavering. "We'll make our luck. Let's get moving."

The group trudged through the rugged mountain trails, the early morning sun casting long shadows over the dense forest. Elias led the way, his movements surprisingly graceful for someone weighed down with so much gear. Erin walked in the middle of the group, flanked protectively by Sarah and Alex. Her glowing eyes scanned the trees ahead, their faint light cutting through the gloom.

Elias spoke over his shoulder, his voice steady but edged with curiosity. "So, MW3746, how much do you remember about your time in Helix Labs?"

Erin flinched slightly at the designation, her gaze dropping to the ground. "Not much," she said softly. "Just flashes. The tests, the pain... being alone."

Sarah stepped forward, her tone sharp. "Her name is Erin. Stop calling her that number like she's some experiment."

Elias turned, his expression neutral. "It's what they called her. It's all I've known her as."

"Well, now you know better," Alex said firmly. "She's not a lab rat or a tool. She's Erin."

Elias raised his hands in mock surrender, a faint smile tugging at the corners of his lips. "Alright, alright. Erin, it is."

Erin gave a small, grateful smile, the tension in her shoulders easing slightly.

As they climbed higher, the air grew thinner and colder, the forest giving way to rocky outcroppings and narrow paths carved into the mountainside. Max glanced at Elias, his curiosity outweighing his usual sarcasm. "So, Elias, how did you even learn about Helix Labs? Doesn't exactly seem like common knowledge."

Elias chuckled. "Let's just say I've always been good at finding things people want to keep hidden. Helix Labs thought they could set up shop out here, and no one would notice, but they didn't count on someone like me poking around."

"You sound almost proud of it," Logan said, his tone skeptical.

"I am," Elias replied without hesitation. "Someone has to shine a light on what they're doing. And now that you kids are involved, I'd say they're finally in over their heads."

The group fell silent momentarily, the gravity of their mission settling over them. Erin broke the silence, her voice quiet but firm. "I don't want anyone else to go through what I did. If stopping the Beacon can stop them, then that's what we have to do."

Alex nodded, his resolve evident. "We're with you, Erin. All the way."

As they neared the Beacon site, the trail leveled out, a massive structure nestled in a clearing at the base of a sheer cliff. The Beacon was a towering metal and glowing crystal spire, its design alien and menacing.

Strange pulses of energy radiated from it, distorting the air around it like a heatwave.

The group crouched behind a line of boulders, their eyes fixed on the structure. Jamari pulled out his PDA, the screen displaying erratic spikes of energy. "This is it," he said. "The Beacon. And it's active."

"Which means we don't have much time," Elias said, scanning the area. "The longer it runs, the more stable the Rift becomes. We have to shut it down before it's too late."

Logan gripped his crowbar, his expression grim. "What's the plan?"

Elias spread a map on the ground, pointing to key points of interest. "There's likely a control room somewhere near the base. That's where we'll find the power source. If we can destroy it, the Beacon should collapse itself."

"And the shadow thing?" Max asked, his voice tinged with fear.

Elias hesitated, then looked at Erin. "That's where she comes in. If it shows up, she's the only one who can hold it off long enough for the rest of us to finish the job."

Erin swallowed hard, but she nodded. "I'll do it."

Alex placed a hand on her shoulder, his voice steady. "We'll be right there with you. We've got your back."

The group exchanged determined looks, each steeling themselves for the fight ahead. As they crept closer to the Beacon, the hum of its energy grew louder, reverberating through the ground beneath their feet. The final confrontation was at hand, and there was no turning back.

Chapter 8: The Beacon Facility

The air inside the facility was stale and oppressive, tinged with a faint metallic tang that made the group's skin crawl. Their flashlights cast narrow beams of light across the walls, revealing corroded metal panels and hastily abandoned equipment. The hum of the Beacon's energy was louder now, a constant vibration that seemed to resonate in their bones.

Elias led the way, his movements confident despite the unfamiliar surroundings. "This place was built to keep people out," he muttered, examining a keypad near a sealed door. "Which means whatever's behind this is important."

"Can you open it?" Alex asked, gripping his crowbar tightly.

Elias smirked, pulling a set of tools from his pack. "Give me a minute."

As Elias worked, the group clustered nearby, their nerves on edge. Erin stood apart, her glowing eyes fixed on the distant, pulsing light visible through the cracks in the walls. She could feel the Beacon's pull, a constant tug at the edge of her mind.

"It's getting stronger," she said softly, her voice almost drowned out by the hum. "We're close."

"Then we've got to move fast," Jamari said, glancing at his PDA. "The energy readings are spiking. If this thing hits full power, we're screwed."

Elias grunted triumphantly as the keypad beeped and the door hissed open. "Got it," he said, stepping aside to let the group through.

The corridor beyond the door was narrower, and the walls were lined with pipes that hissed and groaned under the strain of the Beacon's energy. The heat was palpable, and beads of sweat formed on their foreheads as they pressed deeper into the facility.

Max lagged, his flashlight flickering. "This place is giving me serious horror movie vibes," he muttered. "Any second now, some mutant lab experiment's gonna jump out and—"

"Max, shut up," Logan said, his voice tense. "You're not helping."

Ahead of them, the corridor opened into a massive chamber. The Beacon loomed in the center, a spire of metal and crystal that pulsed with an otherworldly light. The hum of its energy was deafening now, the vibrations so intense that the floor seemed to tremble beneath their feet.

"There it is," Elias said, his voice low. "The heart of the operation."

The group fanned out, their eyes scanning the room for any movement. Jamari's PDA emitted a soft chime as he mapped the area. "Control panels are on the far side," he said, pointing to a row of consoles embedded in the wall. "That's where we'll find the shutdown sequence."

"And the power source?" Alex asked.

Elias pointed to the base of the Beacon, where a cluster of glowing conduits fed into the floor. "There. Destroy that, and we take the whole thing down."

"Sounds easy," Logan said sarcastically. "What's the catch?"

A low growl echoed through the chamber as if in answer, sending a chill down their spines. The shadows at the room's edges seemed to shift and writhe, taking on ominous shapes. Erin's glowing eyes flared as she stepped forward, her voice steady despite the fear in her expression.

"It's here," she said. "The shadow entity."

The group froze, their weapons at the ready as the growls grew louder. From the darkness, the entity emerged, its massive form twisting and undulating as it advanced. Its glowing red eyes locked onto Erin, a guttural snarl reverberating through the chamber.

"We don't have time for this," Elias said sharply. "Jamari, get to the consoles. The rest of you, hold it off."

"Hold it off?" Max repeated, his voice rising in panic. "Are you kidding me?"

"Just do it!" Alex shouted, stepping between the entity and the others. "Erin, can you..."

"I'll try," Erin said, her voice firm as she raised her hands. The glow in her eyes intensified, and the air around her seemed to ripple with energy.

As Jamari sprinted toward the consoles, the others formed a defensive line in front of Erin. The entity roared, its massive limbs lashing out as it charged. Logan swung his crowbar, the impact sending a shockwave through his arms but barely slowing the creature.

"This thing's unstoppable!" he shouted, dodging another strike.

"Not for long," Erin said through gritted teeth. A wave of blue energy erupted from her hands, colliding with the entity and forcing it back. The creature let out an enraged shriek, its form flickering and distorting under the assault.

"Keep it up!" Sarah called, swinging a length of pipe to drive the creature away from Jamari.

At the consoles, Jamari worked frantically, his fingers flying over the controls. "Almost there," he muttered, sweat dripping onto the screen as he bypassed the final layers of security.

The entity lunged at Erin, its massive form bearing down on her. She screamed, releasing another burst of energy that sent it reeling but left her staggering, the glow in her eyes dimming.

"She's weakening," Alex said, catching her as she collapsed. "We need to end this now!"

Jamari's PDA beeped, and the consoles lit up with red warnings. "Got it!" he shouted. "Shutting it down!"

The Beacon's pulsing light faltered, and its energy hum became erratic. The conduits at its base sparked violently, and the ground shook as the entire facility groaned under the strain.

Elias grabbed a bundle of explosives from his pack, tossing them to Logan. "Set these at the base. We'll make sure it never powers back up."

Logan nodded, sprinting toward the Beacon as the rest of the group covered him. The entity let out a final, furious roar, its form unraveling into a mass of writhing shadows before dissipating completely.

Logan planted the explosives and ran back to the group. "Done! Let's move!"

The group bolted for the exit, the facility collapsing as the Beacon overloaded. They burst into the open air just as a loud explosion rocked the mountainside, the shockwave knocking them to the ground.

The group lay sprawled on the rocky ground, catching their breath as the echoes of the explosion faded into the mountain air. A heavy silence followed, broken only by the crackling of fires in the rubble and the occasional debris shift.

"We did it," Sarah murmured, her voice tinged with disbelief. "It's gone."

Alex pushed himself up, his gaze fixed on the smoldering ruins. "Maybe," he said, his tone cautious. "Let's not assume anything yet."

The ground beneath them began to tremble as if in response to his words. It was subtle at first, barely more than a vibration, but it quickly grew into a deep, rhythmic rumble that seemed to emanate from the remains of the facility.

"What now?" Max groaned, clutching his flashlight tightly.

"Get to cover!" Elias barked, ushering them toward a thick patch of brush nearby. The group scrambled for shelter, their eyes locked on the ruins as the tremors intensified.

They watched in stunned silence from their hiding spot as the rubble shifted and rose. Metal beams twisted back into place, shattered walls reassembled themselves, and the ground seemed to heal where it had cracked. The facility wasn't just repairing itself—it was rebuilt, piece by piece, as though rewinding time.

"What the hell is happening?" Logan demanded, his voice low but urgent.

"It's not natural," Elias said grimly. "This isn't just technology. This is Rift Energy. The Beacon... it's regenerating itself."

"How do we stop it?" Sarah asked, her knuckles white as she gripped Erin's hand. The young mutant stirred slightly, her glowing eyes fluttering open but still unfocused.

Elias shook his head. "We might not be able to. Not without more firepower than we've got."

The last piece of the facility snapped into place with a metallic clang, and the rumbling ceased. For a moment, there was an eerie stillness, broken only by the group's ragged breathing. Then, from the center of the facility, a light appeared.

It wasn't like any light they had seen before. It pulsed with an otherworldly intensity, shifting colors in ways that defied logic. The light grew, expanding upward in a brilliant column that pierced the sky, illuminating the surrounding forest in surreal hues. It glowed for what felt like an eternity but was, in reality, only a minute.

"What is that?" Jamari whispered, his PDA emitting frantic beeps as it struggled to process the energy signature.

Erin stirred again, her voice barely audible. "The Rift... it's reaching out."

Before anyone could respond, the light contracted violently, collapsing in on itself as though being sucked into an unseen void. The sky went dark instantly, and the Beacon's glow disappeared entirely. The facility stood silent and whole as though nothing had happened.

"This isn't over," Alex said, his voice steady despite the fear in his eyes. "Not even close."

Erin sat up suddenly, her glowing eyes wide and unfocused as she stared toward the rebuilt facility. Her movements were mechanical, almost like an invisible force was pulling her.

"Erin, wait!" Sarah called, grabbing her arm. But Erin shook her off, her voice distant and hollow.

"I have to go," she said. "It's calling me. The Rift... it's open."

Alex stepped in front of her, blocking her path. "We just destroyed that thing," he said firmly. "You can't go back in there."

Erin's glowing eyes met his, and a desperate flicker crossed her face. "I need to see it. If I don't, we'll never understand what we're dealing with."

Elias put a hand on Alex's shoulder, his expression grim. "She's right. If the Rift is open, we must know what's on the other side. But we're not letting her go alone."

Reluctantly, Alex nodded. The group formed a protective circle around Erin as they moved toward the facility. The air seemed heavier now, charged with an energy that made their skin tingle. The metallic hum of the Beacon had been replaced by an eerie silence, broken only by the sound of their footsteps echoing through the corridors.

Inside, the facility was unrecognizable. The walls shimmered faintly, as if made of liquid metal, and strange symbols pulsed with light along the floors and ceilings. The air was warmer, almost stifling, and the faint scent of ozone hung heavy.

"This place... it's different," Logan said, his grip tightening on his crowbar. "It's like it rebuilt itself into something else."

"The Rift's influence," Elias muttered, eyes scanning the surreal environment. "It's transforming the facility. This isn't just a lab anymore. It's... part of the Rift."

They followed Erin through the twisting corridors, the path ahead illuminated by the faint glow of her eyes. Finally, they reached a massive chamber where the Rift pulsed with an otherworldly light. It hung like a living wound, swirling with colors that seemed impossible to describe. Through the Rift, they could see another world—a landscape of jagged mountains and glowing rivers, with skies that shifted constantly between darkness and light.

The group stared in stunned silence; the sheer impossibility of what they saw rendered them speechless. Jamari's PDA beeped wildly, and the screen flashed error messages while processing the energy signature.

"This... this is impossible," Sarah whispered, her voice trembling.

Elias stepped forward, his eyes fixed on the Rift. "Or maybe we were wrong," he said, his voice heavy with realization. "Destroying the Beacon didn't close the Rift. It opened it."

"So what do we do now?" Max asked, his usual sarcasm absent. "Because I don't think 'smash it with a crowbar' will work this time."

Erin approached the Rift, her expression unreadable. The swirling energy reflected in her glowing eyes as she reached out a hand, stopping just short of touching the edge. "It feels... familiar," she said softly. "Like it's part of me."

Alex grabbed her wrist, pulling her back. "Don't," he said firmly. "We don't know what'll happen if you touch it."

Elias turned to the group, his expression grave. "We need to decide. Do we try to close it? Or do we see what's on the other side?"

The group exchanged uneasy glances, the weight of the decision bearing down on them. The Rift pulsed again, its light casting their faces in shifting hues. For the first time, they felt genuinely uncertain about what lay ahead and whether they were ready to face it.

The group stood in the shadow of the Rift, the swirling portal bathing them in its unearthly light. The tension in the air was thick, the magnitude of the moment weighing heavily on them.

Max broke the silence, his voice cutting through the stillness. "Okay, before we do anything—and I mean anything—can we agree on one thing? We must name whatever's on the other side of that... thing."

Alex frowned, turning to him. "Name it? Are you serious right now?"

"Dead serious," Max replied, crossing his arms. "We can't keep calling it 'the other side.' That's lazy and boring. If we're about to deal with it, we should give it a cool name."

Logan chuckled, stepping closer to the edge of the chamber. "You know, for once, Max has a point. 'The other side' doesn't exactly scream 'epic adventure.'" He tilted his head, a mischievous grin spreading across his face. "How about we call it Phyrexia? Like the creepy, weird world from Magic: The Gathering."

Max snapped his fingers, pointing at Logan. "Yes! Phyrexia. That's perfect. It's ominous, nerdy, and fits the vibe of this nightmare scenario."

"Seriously?" Sarah said, raising an eyebrow. "You want to name a literal otherworldly dimension after a trading card game?"

"Do you have a better idea?" Max shot back, grinning.

Sarah sighed, shaking her head. "Fine. Phyrexia it is."

Elias smirked, glancing at the swirling Rift. "Well, if nothing else, it'll make the history books sound interesting."

Erin, still transfixed by the Rift, didn't respond. Her glowing eyes flickered faintly, and she stepped closer to the edge. "Phyrexia," she whispered, testing the name. "If that's what we're calling it... then what happens if we go there?"

Alex put a hand on her shoulder, pulling her back gently. "We're not going anywhere until we figure out what this thing is doing. Elias, any ideas?"

Elias rubbed his chin thoughtfully, his gaze fixed on the portal. "If the Rift is open, it's not just a doorway. It's a connection. And connections work both ways. Whatever's over there can see us just as clearly as we can see it."

The group exchanged uneasy glances, the gravity of Elias's words sinking in. The Rift pulsed again, its light casting eerie shadows across their faces.

"So what do we do?" Sarah asked, her voice tinged with fear.

"We figure out if we can close it," Elias said. "But if we can't, we might have to go through and deal with whatever's waiting on the other side."

The group fell silent, their eyes fixed on the swirling Rift. For the first time, the enormity of their situation felt truly real. Phyrexia loomed before them, an unknown world filled with untold dangers—and perhaps, answers.

The Rift pulsed once or twice, and a new sound filled the chamber—a low, guttural growl sending shivers down their spines. The swirling light of the Rift began to distort, and shadowy figures emerged, their forms shifting and writhing as though struggling to manifest in this world entirely.

"Uh, guys?" Max said, his voice cracking. "I think we've got company."

The first creature stepped forward, its body an unsettling amalgamation of jagged limbs and translucent skin that pulsed with the same eerie light as the Rift. Its glowing red eyes fixed on the group, and it let out a shriek that reverberated through the chamber.

"Fall back!" Alex shouted, raising his crowbar defensively.

"How many are there?" Logan yelled, swinging his weapon as another creature slithered into view, its movements unnaturally fluid.

"Does it matter?" Jamari shouted, grabbing Erin's arm. "We're out of here!"

The group turned and ran, the creatures hot on their heels. The sound of claws scraping against metal and inhuman growls filled the air, spurring them faster through the surreal, shifting corridors of the facility. Erin stumbled, but Sarah caught her, pulling her forward as they raced toward the exit.

"Elias, any bright ideas?" Alex barked as they sprinted through the twisting halls.

Elias was panting but managed a grim chuckle. "Just one: run faster!"

They burst out into the open air, the cool night a stark contrast to the oppressive heat of the facility. The group didn't stop to look back; their focus was on putting as much distance between themselves and the Rift as possible. The creatures' guttural roars echoed behind them, but the sounds gradually faded as they plunged deeper into the forest.

When they reached Elias's cabin, their lungs burned, and their legs felt like lead. The group collapsed onto the porch, gasping for breath as the night fell silent.

"Is everyone okay?" Sarah asked, her voice trembling.

"Define okay," Max muttered, leaning against the doorframe.

Elias opened the cabin door, motioning them inside. "You can stay here," he said. "It's not much, but it's safe for now."

Alex shook his head, his expression resolute. "Thanks, but we're heading back to Shadowridge. We need to regroup and figure out what to do next."

"Back to the barn?" Elias asked, raising an eyebrow.

"It's our base," Jamari said. "We've got supplies there, and it's close enough to town if we need anything."

Elias nodded reluctantly. "Fair enough. But you're not just dealing with Helix Labs anymore. Whatever came through that Rift, it's only the beginning."

"We know," Alex said grimly. "And that's why we have to stop it."

The group exchanged determined glances before gathering their gear and heading out into the night. The path back to Shadowridge stretched before them, the distant glow of the town a beacon of familiarity in the face of the unknown. They didn't speak much as they walked, their thoughts heavy with the enormity of what lay ahead.

As they approached the outskirts of the forest, Erin glanced back toward the mountains, her glowing eyes narrowing. She didn't say anything, but the pull of the Rift lingered in the back of her mind, a constant reminder that their battle was far from over.

Chapter 9: The Creatures of the Rift

The barn was quieter than usual, the group's usual banter replaced with the weight of what they had just experienced. The faint creak of the rafters and the distant hum of cicadas were the only sounds as they gathered around the table, Jamari's PDA and a stack of files spread out before them.

Erin sat apart from the group, her knees drawn to her chest as she stared toward the mountains. Her glowing eyes were dimmer than usual, her expression unreadable.

"She hasn't said a word since we got back," Sarah whispered to Alex, glancing at Erin.

"She's processing," Alex replied quietly. "We all are. Give her time."

Jamari tapped away at his PDA, his brow furrowed in concentration. "Nothing in these files directly mentions those creatures," he said, frustration creeping into his voice. "But there are notes about Rift energy affecting biological matter. Mutations, destabilizations..."

"What kind of mutations?" Logan asked, leaning over the table.

Jamari picked up a file and flipped it open, pointing to a hastily scribbled note in the margin. "Things like enhanced aggression, increased size, and..." He paused, his face paling slightly. "Total loss of autonomy. It's like the Rift turns them into... I don't know, extensions of itself."

"Great," Max said, throwing up his hands. "So not only do we have to deal with these things, but they're walking Rift zombies?"

"Not zombies," Elias said from his seat by the barn door, his tone thoughtful. "More like guardians. The Rift isn't just a portal; it's a presence. And if it feels threatened, it defends itself."

Sarah frowned, crossing her arms. "Defends itself from what? We weren't trying to attack it."

"Doesn't matter," Elias said, shrugging. "To the Rift, you being there was enough of a threat."

"Then how do we stop it?" Alex asked, his voice firm. "If it's just going to keep defending itself, how do we even get close enough to shut it down?"

Elias leaned back, his gaze shifting to Erin. "That might be where she comes in."

The group turned to Erin, who didn't react at first. Finally, she spoke, her voice soft but steady. "I've seen them before."

Sarah blinked. "The creatures?"

Erin nodded, her glowing eyes flickering faintly. "When I was in the lab. They kept some of them... in tanks. They said they were studying them, but I think they were trying to control them." She paused, her hands clenching into fists. "They couldn't."

"That tracks," Jamari said, flipping to another page in the file. "There are reports here about containment breaches. Helix Labs tried to use Rift energy to create weapons, but things went sideways. Big surprise."

"So these things are their fault," Logan said, his jaw tightening. "They opened the Rift, and now we're stuck cleaning up their mess."

Erin finally turned to face the group, her glowing eyes meeting Alex's. "If they couldn't control them, what makes us think we can stop them?"

Alex hesitated, then placed a hand on her shoulder. "Because we have something they didn't," he said. "We have you. And we're in this together."

Erin nodded slowly, her expression softening. "Then we need a plan. Those creatures won't stop until the Rift is closed."

Jamari glanced at his PDA, then back at the files. "I'll keep digging. If there's anything here about how to counteract the Rift's influence, I'll find it."

"Good," Alex said, standing. "Because if those things come to Shadowridge, we must be ready."

The group fell silent again, the weight of their situation settling over them. Erin turned back to the window, her gaze fixed on the distant mountains and the invisible pull of the Rift beyond. For the first time, she felt something new: hope.

Jamari's fingers flew over his PDA, his brow furrowed in frustration as he combed through files and cross-referenced data. The faint glow of the screen illuminated his face as he muttered under his breath.

"Anything?" Alex asked, leaning over his shoulder.

Jamari sighed. "There's much technical jargon but nothing concrete about what the Rift is or how to stop it. Just theories and failed experiments." He paused, scrolling through another document. "Wait... there's a mention here of a core energy source. It says the Rift might have..." He trailed off, squinting at the screen. "...a central node? But it doesn't explain what that means."

"A central node?" Logan repeated, his tone skeptical. "What are we supposed to do with that? Pull the plug?"

Erin, sitting silently by the window, suddenly spoke up. "I'm starting to remember more," she said, her voice soft but steady.

The group turned to her, their expressions a mix of curiosity and concern.

"What do you mean?" Sarah asked, kneeling beside her.

Erin's glowing eyes flickered as she searched for the right words. "When I was in the lab, they... connected me to the Rift. I saw things, felt things. It's blurry, but it's coming back to me. Maybe... maybe if you could see what I saw, it would help."

"See what you saw?" Max asked, raising an eyebrow. "How does that work?"

"I can show you," Erin said, her gaze meeting Alex's. "But I need you to trust me."

Alex nodded without hesitation. "We trust you, Erin. Do what you need to do."

Erin stood, the faint glow in her eyes intensifying as she raised her hands. The air around her seemed to ripple, and a soft hum filled the barn. "This might feel... strange," she warned.

The group exchanged nervous glances but stood together, bracing themselves. A wave of energy emanated from Erin, enveloping them in a warm, pulsating light. Their surroundings blurred and faded, replaced by a vivid landscape of shifting colors and strange, distorted shapes.

They were no longer in the barn. The group stood in a vast, surreal expanse that defied logic. The ground beneath them shimmered like liquid glass, and the sky above was a swirling canvas of impossible colors. Towering, alien structures loomed in the distance, their forms pulsating with energy.

"Where are we?" Sarah whispered, her voice trembling.

"This is what I saw when they connected me to the Rift," Erin said, her voice echoing slightly in the strange space. "It's not real... not exactly. It's more like... a memory of the Rift."

"A memory?" Jamari asked, his curiosity piqued. "This place looks alive."

"It is," Erin replied. "The Rift isn't just energy. It's a presence, a consciousness. And it's watching us."

The group tensed as the ground beneath them rippled, forming a pathway that led toward a massive, pulsating structure in the distance. The structure radiated a sense of power and unease, its surface shifting and morphing as if alive.

"What's that?" Logan asked, pointing toward the structure.

"The core," Erin said, her voice almost a whisper. "The central node Jamari mentioned. That's what they were trying to reach."

Elias stepped forward, his eyes narrowing as he studied the structure. "If that's the source of the Rift's power, it's also our target. But getting to it isn't going to be easy."

Suddenly, the air around them darkened, and a low growl reverberated through the space. Shadowy figures began to emerge from the edges of the memory, their forms shifting and twisting like the creatures they had encountered before.

"They're here," Erin said, her voice filled with dread. "Even in my memories, they're here."

"Then we fight," Alex said, approaching her. "If there's anything in these memories that can help us, we will find it. Together."

The group formed a defensive circle around Erin, their determination shining despite the surreal and terrifying landscape. As the shadow creatures advanced, Erin's glow intensified, and the memory shifted again, pulling them deeper into her connection with the Rift.

The surreal memory began to shift, the vibrant landscape twisting into something more mechanical and sterile. The colors faded into muted tones of gray and white, and the alien structures gave way to the cold, clinical environment of Helix Labs. The group stood in what appeared to be a massive laboratory, its walls lined with tanks filled with shadowy figures suspended in a viscous, glowing liquid.

Jamari's voice broke the tense silence as he pointed toward a nearby console, its screen flickering with data lines. "Wait. This is... I've seen this before in the files we recovered. These tanks... they weren't for creating the creatures."

"What do you mean?" Alex asked, his grip tightening on the crowbar in his hands as his eyes darted between the tanks.

Jamari moved to the console, his fingers rushing across the keyboard. The screen displayed a series of reports, diagrams, and genetic sequences. "Helix Labs weren't creating the creatures. They were coming through the Rift from Phyrexia. Helix Labs captured them and... tested them."

"Tested them?" Sarah repeated, her voice tinged with disgust. "For what?"

Jamari's face darkened as he scrolled through the files. "Their DNA. Helix Labs was extracting their genetic material and splicing it with human DNA to create mutant weapons. They weren't trying to stop the Rift. They were exploiting it."

Erin stepped closer to the tanks, her glowing eyes reflecting in the glass. The shadowy figure inside twitched slightly, its distorted form barely recognizable as anything natural. "They were using them," she said softly. "And using us."

Logan slammed his crowbar against a nearby metal counter, echoing through the memory. "Unbelievable. They weren't just experimenting on these things—they were weaponizing them. For what? To sell to the highest bidder?"

"For the government," Elias said grimly. He stepped beside Jamari, his eyes scanning the console. "These reports talk about contracts and military applications. Helix Labs wasn't working in the shadows just for profit. They were developing bioweapons under the guise of national security."

Sarah's fists clenched at her sides. "So all of this—the Rift, the creatures, Erin...—it's all because they wanted weapons?"

"Pretty much," Jamari said, his voice laced with anger. "And from what I can tell, they weren't very good at controlling what they were creating. That's why there were so many containment breaches. The creatures fought back."

Max let out a hollow laugh, shaking his head. "Great. So not only are we dealing with an interdimensional nightmare, but we've also got Helix Labs playing mad scientist and making it worse."

Erin took a step back from the tank, her expression unreadable. "They made me from this," she said quietly, gesturing toward the shadowy figure inside. "Part human, part Rift."

Alex placed a hand on her shoulder. "You're more than that, Erin. You're not their experiment anymore. You're with us."

Erin nodded slowly, her glowing eyes meeting his. "Then we need to stop them. Not just the Rift but Helix Labs. All of it."

Jamari turned back to the group, his expression resolute. "If we can find a way to shut down their research and close the Rift for good, we can end this. But we need to figure out how to sever their connection to Phyrexia. Otherwise, they'll keep opening it."

The memory began to fade, the sterile lab dissolving into darkness. The group found themselves back in the barn, the warm glow of the lanterns starkly contrasting with the cold, harsh environment they had just witnessed. Erin staggered slightly, and Sarah caught her, guiding her to sit.

"We have a lot to figure out," Alex said, his voice firm. "But at least now we know the truth. Helix Labs is the real enemy, and we will take them down."

The group sat in a tense circle, the air in the barn thick with urgency as they tried to make sense of their next steps. Jamari's revelation about Helix Labs weighed heavily on them, but it also gave them clarity: they now had a target.

"Alright," Alex began, his tone firm, "we know Helix Labs is the source of all this. They opened the Rift and brought those creatures here. They have been experimenting on Erin, and who knows how many others there are? If we're going to stop this, we must hit them where it hurts."

"And where exactly is that?" Logan asked, leaning back against a stack of hay. "It's not like they gave us a map to their evil lair."

Jamari tapped on his PDA, pulling up the files they had recovered earlier. "We might have a lead. These reports mention a main facility—a place where the experiments started. If we can find it, we might be able to shut everything down at the source."

"But what about the Rift?" Sarah asked, glancing at Erin. "Even if we stop Helix Labs, the Rift is still open. Creatures are still coming through."

Erin, who had been silent since their return to the barn, finally spoke. "If we can get to the main facility, we might find a way to sever the connection. The Rift is tied to their technology. If we destroy that, we might be able to close it for good."

Max groaned, rubbing his temples. "Great. So we have to break into a super-secret government lab, destroy their world-ending tech, and close an interdimensional portal. Easy peasy."

Sarah shot him a look. "We've done crazier things."

"True," Max conceded with a grin. "But this one's definitely top of the list."

Elias's name came up as they discussed their plan, and Alex stood pacing the barn. "We need Elias's input on this," he said. "He knows more about Helix Labs than anyone. If we pull this off, we'll need his help."

"Are we sure he'll go along with it?" Logan asked. "He's a bit... unpredictable."

"Unpredictable or not, he wants to take Helix Labs down as much as we do," Alex replied. "Let's head back to his cabin and fill him in. The sooner we move, the better."

The group arrived at Elias's cabin just as the first rays of dawn began to break over the horizon. The old man was already awake, tinkering with a strange device on his porch. He looked up as they approached, his expression shifting from curiosity to concern as he saw their serious faces.

"Back so soon?" Elias asked, setting the device aside. "I take it you found something."

"We found out everything," Alex said, stepping forward. "Helix Labs isn't just opening the Rift. They capture creatures from the other side and use their DNA to create weapons. Erin... she's one of their experiments."

Elias's eyes narrowed as he processed the information. "Figures," he muttered. "I always suspected they were up to something worse than just studying the Rift. But using it to create bioweapons? That's a new level of evil."

"We think their main facility might hold the key to shutting it all down," Jamari said, holding up his PDA. "We found some coordinates in the files. If we can get in there and destroy their tech, we might be able to sever the Rift connection."

Elias rubbed his chin, his gaze distant. "It's a solid plan," he said after a moment. "But you'll need more than good intentions to pull it off. Their main facility is bound to be heavily guarded. And if the Rift's energy is as unstable as you describe, you'll fight more than just agents."

"We don't have a choice," Erin said, her voice steady. "This has to end."

Elias nodded, a faint smile tugging at the corners of his lips. "I like your resolve, kid. Alright, count me in. I've got some old maps and a few tricks that might help. If we're going to take Helix Labs down, we're doing it right."

The group exchanged determined looks, their fear tempered by a renewed sense of purpose. For the first time since this nightmare began, they had a clear path forward.

"Let's gear up and get ready," Alex said. "We've got a long road ahead of us."

Max leaned against the cabin wall, arms crossed with an exaggeratedly thoughtful look. "Okay, before we go storming into the belly of the beast, I have an important suggestion."

Alex raised an eyebrow, already skeptical. "What now?"

Max straightened up, a grin spreading across his face. "Pizza. We need pizza. And I'm not just saying that because I'm starving. Think about it: we'll take on some interdimensional nightmare fuel and a shadowy government lab. Don't we deserve one last slice of normal before we dive into that mess?"

Logan chuckled, shaking his head. "You know, for once, I agree with you."

Sarah sighed but smiled. "As much as I hate to admit it, he's got a point. We could all use a break. And some carbs."

Jamari grinned, closing his PDA. "I'm in. Besides, maybe a little downtime will help us think clearer."

Elias snorted from his spot by the barn door. "Fine. Get your pizza. Just don't forget we've got a world to save when you're done."

The familiar neon lights of the Pizza Palace felt like a breath of fresh air after everything the group had been through. The smell of melted cheese and warm dough filled the air as they slid into their usual booth, and the din of arcade games and laughter provided a comforting backdrop.

"Large pepperoni?" Max asked, already pulling out a handful of quarters for the arcade machines.

"Of course," Alex said, relaxing for the first time in what felt like days. "And don't forget breadsticks."

While waiting for their food, the group dispersed to their favorite games. Logan and Max took on the racing machines, their competitive shouts drawing attention from a few other patrons. Sarah and Jamari gravitated toward the pinball machines while Alex leaned against the counter, watching Erin. She stood before an old claw machine, her glowing eyes reflecting the bright colors inside.

"Ever played one of these?" Alex asked, stepping beside her.

Erin shook her head, her voice soft. "No. What do you do?"

Alex grinned, dropping a coin into the slot. "You try to grab one of the prizes with the claw. It's harder than it looks, but it's fun."

Erin watched Alex maneuvering the claw, carefully positioning it over a small plush toy. The claw descended, gripping the toy before slipping and dropping it. Erin's expression softened, a faint smile tugging at her lips.

"Let me try," she said.

Alex handed her a coin, and Erin surprisingly mimicked his movements. The claw latched onto a small stuffed alien and managed to hold on, dropping it into the chute.

"I did it," she said, her smile widening as she picked up the toy.

"See? You've got the touch," Alex said, smiling back.

The group reconvened at the booth when the pizza arrived, laughing and sharing stories between bites. For a moment, it was as if the world outside didn't exist—no Rift, no Helix Labs, no creatures: just friends, pizza, and the glow of arcade games.

"Alright," Alex said as they finished the last slice. "Break time's over. Let's head back and get to work."

Max groaned dramatically but stood up. "Fine. But next time we save the world, I'm picking the post-mission meal."

The group emerged from the Pizza Palace, their spirits lifted momentarily by the laughter and warmth shared over their meal. The neon lights of the restaurant flickered behind them as they stepped onto the quiet streets of Shadowridge, the cool night air bringing a sobering reminder of the task ahead.

"I have to admit," Max said, stuffing his hands into his jacket pockets, "this was a solid idea. Pizza makes everything slightly less terrible."

"Let's hope it's enough to fuel us for what's coming," Alex replied, glancing at Erin. She walked quietly beside Sarah, the stuffed alien from the claw machine tucked under her arm.

As they turned a corner, the atmosphere shifted. Parked just ahead, three black SUVs with tinted windows sat idling under the streetlights. Two men in dark suits leaned against one of the vehicles, their postures casual but watchful. The group slowed instinctively, exchanging wary glances.

"Friends of yours?" Logan muttered, his voice low.

"Nope," Alex said sharply, his eyes narrowing.

One of the men straightened, his gaze locking onto the group. His tall, lean frame was sharp in the dim light, and his presence exuded authority. The man's graying hair and cold, calculating eyes seemed to take in everything at once.

"Dr. Victor Henshaw," Elias muttered under his breath, his tone grim. "This just got complicated."

Henshaw stepped forward, his expression unreadable. "Alexander Carson and company, I presume?" His voice was smooth, with an edge of condescension. "I was hoping we'd meet under less... inconvenient circumstances."

"Who's asking?" Alex replied, his tone defensive.

"I'm Dr. Victor Henshaw," the man said, pulling a badge from his pocket and holding it up. "FBI. But more importantly, I represent the interests of Helix Labs. And you, all of you, have something—or someone—that belongs to us." His cold gaze shifted to Erin, who flinched slightly but held her ground.

"She doesn't belong to anyone," Sarah snapped, stepping protectively before Erin. "She's not your experiment anymore."

Henshaw's lips curled into a faint smile but didn't reach his eyes. "That's a noble sentiment but naive. You have no idea what you're dealing with. The Rift is a threat beyond your comprehension, and she"—he pointed at Erin—"is its most dangerous piece. You think you're helping her but endangering everyone around you."

"That's rich, coming from the people who created her," Logan growled. "And who opened the Rift in the first place."

Henshaw's expression hardened. "You misunderstand. Everything we've done has been for the greater good. Containing the Rift and its anomalies is the only way to ensure the safety of this world. She's a key part of that containment."

Erin stepped forward, her glowing eyes meeting Henshaw's unflinching gaze. "You're lying," she said quietly. "You didn't want to contain the Rift. You wanted to control it. And you wanted to control me."

Henshaw's jaw tightened, but he didn't deny it. "You can believe whatever you like. But the fact remains: you're a danger to yourself and everyone around you. Come with me willingly, and I promise you'll be treated fairly."

"Yeah, because that worked out so well for her last time," Max said, sarcasm dripping from his words. "Hard pass."

Henshaw's gaze shifted to Elias. "And you. I should've known you'd be involved. Always meddling, always stirring up trouble. Don't think I've forgotten about your little escapades."

Elias smirked, unfazed. "I live to disappoint you, Victor."

Henshaw sighed, his tone cooling. "This is your last chance. Turn her over, or there will be consequences."

Alex stepped forward, his voice steady but full of resolve. "She's with us. And we're not letting you take her."

Henshaw studied the group briefly, then nodded to his agents. "Very well. But don't think this is over. We'll find you again; it won't be a negotiation next time."

As the agents moved toward the SUVs, Henshaw lingered momentarily, his sharp gaze fixing on Erin. "You can't run forever, MW3746. Sooner or later, you'll realize we're your only option."

The vehicles pulled away, leaving the group standing in tense silence. Erin clutched the stuffed alien tighter, her glowing eyes dim as she avoided everyone's gaze.

"Well," Max said finally, his attempt at levity failing to mask the tension. "That was fun. What's next?"

Alex looked around at his friends, his determination unwavering. "We keep going. We'll figure out how to stop Helix Labs, the Rift, and Henshaw. No matter what it takes."

The group walked in tense silence, the sound of their footsteps echoing faintly on the empty streets. The encounter with Henshaw had shaken them but also fueled their resolve.

They gathered at the barn around the makeshift table littered with maps, files, and Jamari's ever-present PDA. The air was thick with purpose as Alex took the lead.

"Alright," he began, his tone decisive. "Henshaw's made it clear he's not going to stop. We must determine our next move before he gets ahead of us."

"If he's even one step behind us, it won't stay that way for long," Elias said, leaning against the wall. "The guy's relentless, and he's got the resources of Helix Labs and the FBI backing him up."

Jamari tapped on his PDA, and his screen displayed the coordinates from the recovered files. "We still have these to check out. If this is their main facility, it's where we'll find the answers we need to shut this whole thing down."

"And a whole lot of trouble," Logan muttered. "If Henshaw's already onto us, it won't be long before they reinforce that place."

"We can't waste time," Alex said firmly. He turned to Erin, who sat quietly, her glowing eyes reflecting the lantern light. "Erin, are you up for this? We're going to need you more than ever."

Erin looked up, her gaze steady despite the weight of his words. "I'm ready," she said softly. "If this is the only way to stop them, I'll do whatever it takes."

Sarah placed a reassuring hand on Erin's shoulder. "We're in this together. No one's facing this alone."

"Alright," Alex said, nodding. "We get some rest tonight, and tomorrow, we head out. It's time to take the fight to Helix Labs."

The group dispersed to their corners of the barn, the tension easing slightly as they prepared for the long road ahead. The stuffed alien sat on a nearby crate, a small reminder of their shared fleeting moments of normalcy. As the lantern light flickered, Erin sat by the window, staring out into the night and toward the mountains where the Rift pulsed faintly in the distance.

Chapter 10: The Barn Emergency

The first rays of morning light filtered through the cracks in the barn walls, casting faint golden streaks across the dusty floor. The group stirred in their makeshift sleeping arrangements, still weary from the tension of the previous day. Erin sat upright against a pile of blankets, her glowing eyes dim as she gazed out the window toward the distant mountains. The faint hum of the Rift lingered in her mind, a reminder of the battle yet to come.

The sudden, frantic knocking on the barn door shattered the morning calm. Everyone jolted awake, their hearts racing as they scrambled to their feet. Alex grabbed a crowbar, gesturing for the others to stay back as he cautiously approached the door.

"Who is it?" Alex called, his voice sharp.

"It's me, Rachel!" came the muffled reply, followed by more desperate knocks. "Open the door! Please, it's Sarah's sister!"

Sarah froze, her face paling as Alex swung the door open to reveal Rachel, a close family friend. She was disheveled, her eyes red and puffy from crying.

"Rachel, what happened?" Sarah asked, rushing forward.

Rachel's voice broke as she spoke. "It's your sister, Ellie. There was a hit-and-run last night. She's in the hospital. It's bad, Sarah."

Sarah's hand flew to her mouth, her eyes welling with tears. "Oh my God. Where is she? Is she going to be okay?"

"She's stable for now," Rachel said quickly, touching Sarah's shoulder. "But they need to run more tests. She's asking for you."

"We'll go right now," Alex said firmly, glancing at the others. "Let's get to the hospital."

The group climbed into Rachel's SUV, and the ride to the hospital was tense and silent. Sarah sat in the passenger seat, her hands clasped tightly in her lap as she stared out the window. Sitting in the back with Alex and Max, Erin watched her quietly, her fears mingling with the heavy atmosphere.

As the hospital came into view, Logan spoke for the first time, his voice low. "You think this was an accident?"

Alex frowned, his gaze hardening. "I don't know. But after last night... it feels like too much of a coincidence."

"You're saying you think the FBI did this?" Max asked, incredulous.

"I'm saying it's suspicious," Alex replied. "Henshaw's desperate to stop us. Hurting someone close to us? That's one way to make us hesitate."

Logan nodded grimly. "If they did, they're watching us more closely than we thought."

The van screeched to a halt in the hospital's parking lot. Sarah was out the door before the engine stopped, rushing into the building with the others close behind.

In the sterile confines of the hospital room, Ellie lay pale and motionless, her left arm in a cast and bandages wrapped around her head. Machines beeped softly, monitoring her condition. Sarah's breath hitched as she approached her sister's bedside, tears streaming down her face.

"Ellie," she whispered, taking her sister's hand. "I'm here."

Ellie's eyes fluttered open, and she managed a faint smile. "Hey, kiddo," she said weakly. "Told you I'd be fine."

Sarah let out a choked laugh; her relief was evident. "You scared me half to death, Ellie."

The rest of the group lingered near the door, giving Sarah and Ellie space while keeping a watchful eye on the hallway. Logan leaned closer to Alex, his voice barely a whisper. "If this was Henshaw's doing, what's stopping him from coming after the rest of us?"

"Nothing," Alex said grimly. "Which is why we need to be careful. And fast."

Erin's glowing eyes flicked toward the hallway, her expression unreadable. She could feel the tension in the air, the unspoken fear that their enemies were closer than they realized. She closed her eyes momentarily, reaching out with her senses, hoping to find answers in the swirling energy she could feel just beyond the edge of perception.

Sarah's voice brought her back to the present. "Thank you," she said, turning to the group. "For coming with me. For being here."

Alex nodded. "We're family, Sarah. We stick together."

Sarah smiled faintly, her resolve hardening. "Then let's make sure this doesn't happen to anyone else. Let's take Henshaw down."

The group lingered in the hospital's waiting area after visiting Ellie. Sarah sat apart from the others, her hands clasped tightly in her lap as she stared at the floor. Alex approached her, pulling up a chair and sitting across from her.

"We'll take care of this," Alex said gently. "Helix Labs, the Rift, Henshaw—whatever it takes."

Sarah looked up, her expression conflicted. "I want to help. I want to go after them. But I can't leave while Ellie's still here. She's stable, but what if something changes? What if she needs me?"

"You don't have to explain," Alex replied. "We're not going anywhere until you're ready. We'll use the time to regroup and refine the plan. We'll ensure there's nothing they can throw at us that we're unprepared for."

The rest of the group nodded in agreement, gathering around. Max leaned against the wall, his arms crossed. "Besides, sticking around means more pizza runs. Win-win."

Sarah managed a small smile at that. "Thanks, everyone. I don't know what I'd do without you."

The group spread their files and notes on the makeshift table at the barn. Jamari was already buried in his PDA, analyzing the data they'd collected from Helix Labs. Logan leaned over a map, marking their identified facility's potential routes and entry points.

"We've got the coordinates," Jamari said, not looking up from his screen. "The files mention a central lab housing their main servers. If we can access those, we might find a way to shut everything down remotely."

"And what about the Rift?" Sarah asked, her tone sharp. "What's stopping them from opening it somewhere else?"

"Good question," Jamari muttered. "We'll need to find their backup plans. Once we crack their servers, we'll know if they've got other sites."

Logan nodded, tracing his finger over the map. "We need to plan for contingencies. If things go south, we'll need an escape route. This isn't just about breaking in—it's about getting out alive."

Alex stood at the head of the table, his gaze sweeping over the group. "Alright. We'll keep working on the plan and tighten it until there's no room for error. And while we're at it, we stay on guard. If Henshaw's watching us, we must be ready for anything."

Erin, seated near the window, spoke up quietly. "The Rift feels... restless. It's like it's waiting for something. If we don't act soon, it might not matter what Helix Labs is planning."

Her words hung heavy in the air, a stark reminder of the stakes they faced. Despite the tension, there was a sense of unity among the group—a determination to face whatever came next together.

The group settled into an unusual routine over the next few days. With Sarah spending most of her time at the hospital visiting her sister, the others took turns accompanying her and finding moments to unwind at the barn. They all agreed that balancing rest and preparation was critical for what lay ahead.

Max, naturally, took charge of organizing "mandatory relaxation sessions." One afternoon, he set up a makeshift movie theater in the barn with an old projector and a stack of VHS tapes he'd borrowed from his house.

"You're all welcome," Max said with a theatrical bow as the opening credits of *Jurassic Park* played on the barn's wall. "This is what heroes do—watch dinosaurs eat people. It's motivational."

Even Alex, usually severe and focused, smiled as they settled in. Erin sat quietly at the edge of the group, watching the movie with wide eyes. Now and then, Logan glanced over at her, noticing how she seemed to relax during the lighthearted moments.

When they weren't relaxing, the group refined their plan. Jamari pored over the data on his PDA, identifying potential weak points in Helix Labs' systems, while Alex and Logan worked on contingency routes. Sarah helped Jamari organize their files and assess the risks when she wasn't at the hospital.

One quiet evening, Erin and Logan found themselves alone in the barn. She sat near the window, absentmindedly running her fingers over the stuffed alien she'd won at the Pizza Palace. Logan, tinkering with an old radio nearby, looked up and hesitated before speaking.

"You know, you're getting pretty good at fitting in," he said with a lopsided grin. "Winning claw machine prizes, quoting *Jurassic Park*... all that."

Erin's glowing eyes flickered as she looked at him. "I'm trying," she said softly. "But it's still hard. Being around all of you feels... different. In a good way. But sometimes I wonder if I belong here."

Logan leaned back against a beam, his expression thoughtful. "You do," he said firmly. "We all have our weird baggage, but that doesn't mean we don't belong. Besides, you're one of us now. Max would be crushed if you left. He'd have no one else to beat at the claw machine."

That earned a small smile from Erin. "Thanks, Logan. That means a lot."

"Anytime," he replied. There was a moment of silence, comfortable yet charged, as they sat together.

Over the days, the barn became a hub of quiet resilience. The group's bonds deepened as they balanced their downtime with the growing urgency of their mission. Alex remained steadfast, leading their efforts with determination. Sarah's time with her sister strengthened her resolve to bring down Helix Labs, while Jamari's precision and ingenuity kept their plans moving forward.

And though Erin often withdrew into moments of quiet contemplation, the group's care and camaraderie made her feel less like an experiment and more like someone who mattered.

The days in Shadowridge were a reprieve, but the looming confrontation with Helix Labs was never far from their minds. Each group member knew that the time for planning and resting would be over soon. And when that time came, they'd be ready.

A week later, Sarah's sister, Ellie, was finally discharged. The group gathered to help Sarah escort her home, their relief palpable as Ellie, though bruised and bandaged, cracked jokes on the ride back.

"You've got to watch out for these hit-and-run drivers," Ellie said wryly, managing a weak grin. "They have no respect for pedestrians or my favorite jacket."

Sarah rolled her eyes, though her expression softened. "I'll get you a new jacket, and you're not walking anywhere alone for a while."

The mood lightened as Ellie settled back into her home, leaving Sarah reassured and able to rejoin the group with renewed focus.

Back at the barn, Jamari stood over his PDA, his face illuminated by its faint glow. "All right, team," he announced, drawing everyone's attention. I've got it. The files I cracked last night gave me the entire layout of the Helix Labs facility. We now know exactly where we need to go: the central server room in Section E. They store all the data we need to shut down their operations and discover what else they've been hiding."

Alex leaned over the table, studying the map Jamari projected. "What's the fastest way in?"

"This maintenance tunnel here," Jamari said, pointing to a red line. "It's underground so that we can avoid most of their exterior security. But it's not without risks. There are cameras and motion sensors we'll need to bypass."

"What about when we're inside?" Logan asked. "The labs are bound to be crawling with agents."

"Exactly," Jamari replied. "We'll need to move fast and stay quiet. If we're caught, we'll never reach the server room."

Max crossed his arms. "Okay, but what happens once we're there? Do we grab the data and run?"

"Not quite," Jamari said. "We're not just looking for data. The facility's systems control their Rift experiments. If we can shut those down, we might be able to sever the Rift's connection to their technology."

Sarah, seated next to Erin, frowned. "And if we don't?"

Jamari hesitated, then said grimly, "If we don't, they'll keep opening it. Again and again. And the creatures will keep coming."

The group fell silent, the weight of the mission settling over them. Finally, Alex straightened, his expression resolute. "Then we make sure we succeed. Jamari, finalize the details. Logan, Max, and I will figure out the gear we need. Sarah, Erin—check our escape routes. If we run into trouble, I want to know every way out of that place."

As they broke into their tasks, Logan lingered near Erin. "You okay?" he asked quietly.

Erin nodded, though her glowing eyes betrayed her unease. "It's just... a lot. But I'm ready."

"You've got this," Logan said with a reassuring smile. "And we've got your back."

Their eyes met for a moment, and Erin managed a small smile. "Thanks, Logan."

That evening, the group gathered around the table one last time to review the plan. Maps, notes, and diagrams were spread out before them, every detail scrutinized.

"This is it," Alex said, looking at each of them. "Tomorrow, we head to Helix Labs. No more delays, no more distractions. We end this."

The group nodded, their determination palpable. Whatever awaited them at Helix Labs, they were ready to face it together.

Chapter 11: Infiltrating Helix Labs

Dawn broke over Shadowridge, painting the sky in streaks of pink and gold. The barn was already alive with activity as the group prepared. Maps were folded and tucked into backpacks, supplies double-checked, and the tension in the air was palpable.

Alex stood by the barn door, his crowbar slung over his shoulder as he scanned the horizon. "Everyone ready?" he asked, his voice steady but firm.

"Ready as we'll ever be," Logan replied, tightening the straps on his pack.

Jamari held up his PDA, the screen displaying a map of the Helix Labs facility. "I've synced the layout to my tracker. We'll know where to go if we can stay quiet."

Sarah adjusted her jacket, a determined look on her face. "We've got this."

Erin hovered near the back of the group, her glowing eyes flickering faintly. Logan caught her gaze and gave her an encouraging nod. "You okay?" he asked.

She hesitated, then nodded. "I just... I know this is going to be dangerous. But I'm ready."

"Good," Logan said with a small smile. "Because we're counting on you."

The group piled into Logan's van, the ride to the facility quiet save for the low hum of the engine. Jamari sat up front, his PDA balanced on his knee as he reviewed their entry route.

"The maintenance tunnel will get us undetected if we move quickly," he explained. "Once inside, we head straight for Section E. That's where the server room is."

"And the agents?" Sarah asked, glancing out the window.

Jamari frowned. "Hopefully, the security patrols won't expect us to enter through the tunnels. But once we're inside, it'll be harder to avoid them."

"We stick to the plan," Alex said firmly. "No unnecessary risks, no splitting up. We're in and out before they even know we're there."

The maintenance tunnel entrance was hidden behind a thicket of trees, concealed by years of overgrowth. Logan cleared the brush away while Alex pried open the rusted hatch, the metal groaning in protest. A damp, musty smell wafted up from the darkness below.

"Lovely," Max muttered, peering into the gloom. "Anybody bring air freshener?"

"Just get moving," Alex said, motioning for Jamari to lead the way.

The group descended into the tunnel, their flashlights cutting through the darkness. The walls were lined with corroded pipes, water dripping steadily from above. Their footsteps echoed eerily, but they pressed on, the map guiding them toward the facility's underground entrance.

Erin paused briefly, her glowing eyes flickering as she glanced behind them. Logan noticed and stopped. "What is it?" he asked in a whisper.

"I don't know," Erin replied, her voice hushed. "It just feels... like we're being watched."

Logan's grip on his crowbar tightened. "Stay close. If something's down here, we'll deal with it together."

The tunnel opened into a dimly lit corridor, and the stark, clinical architecture of Helix Labs was immediately recognizable. Jamari checked his PDA, and the screen displayed their location.

"We're in," he said. "Server room is two floors up. There's a freight elevator around the corner."

Alex nodded. "Let's move."

They crept through the corridor, their footsteps muffled on the polished floors. The hum of machinery filled the air, along with the occasional murmur of voices in the distance. As they reached the elevator, Jamari quickly accessed the control panel, bypassing the security lock.

"Got it," he whispered as the elevator doors slid open.

The group stepped inside, their nerves taut as the elevator ascended. Erin stood in the corner, her hands clenched into fists as she focused on the faint pull of the Rift's energy somewhere above them.

The elevator dinged softly, and the doors opened to reveal Section E's sterile, white walls. The group stepped out, their senses on high alert as they moved toward the server room.

But before they could reach their destination, a sharp voice echoed down the hall.

"Intruders! Stop right there!"

Alex turned to see a group of agents led by Dr. Victor Henshaw. His cold, calculating gaze locked onto Erin.

"I told you," Henshaw said, his tone icy. "You can't run forever."

"Run!" Alex shouted, and the group scattered as the agents advanced, the sound of alarms blaring through the facility.

The group scattered, their movements swift and calculated despite the chaos. Alex led the charge down the nearest corridor; his crowbar gripped tightly in one hand as alarms blared around them. Behind him, Sarah and Max followed closely, their breaths coming in quick, shallow bursts.

"Jamari, which way?" Alex called over the noise, glancing back at their tech wizard, frantically tapping his PDA.

"Left! Then two doors down on the right," Jamari shouted, his voice strained. "The server room should be there!"

"Got it," Alex said, waving the others forward. "Let's go!"

Meanwhile, Erin and Logan veered off in the opposite direction, taking cover in a side corridor to avoid the approaching agents. Erin's glowing eyes flickered brightly, a sign of her heightened stress.

"They're closing in," Logan said, gripping his crowbar tightly. "We can't stay here for long."

"I can hold them off," Erin said, her voice steady but tinged with apprehension. "You go help the others."

"Not a chance," Logan replied firmly. "We do this together. Always."

Erin hesitated, then nodded, a flicker of gratitude crossing her face. "Okay. But if it gets bad... I'll do what I must."

Footsteps echoed down the hallway, and Logan motioned for Erin to stay low. As the first agent rounded the corner, Logan lunged forward, his crowbar swinging in a precise arc that knocked the man's weapon aside. Erin stepped in, a pulse of blue energy emanating from her hands and sending the agent sprawling back.

Alex and the others had managed to breach the door in the server room, barricading it behind them as Jamari worked feverishly at the main terminal. The room was bathed in a cold, fluorescent light, rows of servers humming ominously around them.

"How much time do you need?" Sarah asked, glancing nervously at the door.

"Five minutes," Jamari said, not looking up. "But that's only if this system doesn't fry my PDA."

"We might not have five minutes," Max muttered, pacing near the barricade. "Those guys will break through any second now."

"We'll hold them off," Alex said, gripping his crowbar and stepping toward the door. "Sarah, you stay here with Jamari. Max, you're with me."

Max groaned but followed, gripping a length of pipe he'd picked up earlier. "Why do I always get the fun jobs?"

The door rattled as the agents began to push against it, the barricade creaking ominously. Alex braced himself, exchanging a determined glance with Max.

"Whatever happens," Alex said, his voice low, "we keep them out. No matter what."

Elsewhere, Erin and Logan continued their battle, the agents falling back as Erin's energy pulses grew more controlled and precise. But the strain was beginning to show—her breathing was labored, and her glow dimmed with each burst of power.

"Erin, you're overdoing it!" Logan shouted, swinging his crowbar to disarm another agent. "You've got to save your strength!"

"I'll be fine," Erin insisted, though her knees wobbled slightly. "We just have to keep them from regrouping."

As the last agents in their immediate vicinity retreated, Logan grabbed Erin's arm, steadying her. "Come on. Let's find the others."

Back in the server room, Jamari's PDA beeped triumphantly. "Got it!" he exclaimed, pulling a floppy disk from the terminal. "I've copied everything—facility layouts, research data, Rift control protocols—you name it."

"Great," Sarah said, relief evident in her voice. "Now, let's get out of here."

The barricade groaned as the agents outside pushed harder, the door beginning to splinter. Alex and Max stood ready, their grips tight on their makeshift weapons.

"Jamari, is there another way out of here?" Alex asked urgently.

"There's an access hatch in the back," Jamari pointedly. "It leads to the maintenance tunnels. But it's going to be a tight fit."

"Then we squeeze," Alex said, motioning for everyone to move. "Go, now!"

Sarah and Jamari crawled through the hatch first, followed by Max. Alex held the door as long as he could, his strength finally giving way as the agents burst through. He dove for the hatch just as a gunshot rang out, narrowly missing him as he disappeared into the tunnel.

The group reunited with Erin and Logan in the maintenance tunnel, their expressions a mix of relief and determination.

"Did you get it?" Logan asked.

"We got it," Jamari confirmed, holding the floppy disk. "Let's get out of here before they catch up."

As the group fled through the twisting tunnels, the alarms above blared, a stark reminder that their mission was far from over. But they had a piece of the puzzle for the first time—something tangible to use against Helix Labs and the Rift.

"Whatever happens next," Alex said as they emerged into the cool night air, "we fight back. And we win."

Chapter 12: Escape and Revelation

The cool night air bit at their faces as the group scrambled out of the maintenance tunnel, their breaths coming in ragged gasps. The entrance they had used to infiltrate Helix Labs now loomed behind them, dark and ominous, the echoes of alarms faint in the distance.

Alex turned to Jamari, who clutched the floppy disk like a lifeline. "What did you get?" he asked, his voice low but urgent.

"Everything," Jamari replied, still catching his breath. "Facility layouts, Rift experiment data, and something labeled 'Project Nexus.' I think it's the key to shutting everything down."

"Project Nexus?" Sarah repeated, frowning. "What's that supposed to mean?"

Jamari shook his head. "I don't know yet, but if it's tied to the Rift, we must figure it out. Fast."

"We don't have time to sort through it now," Alex said, scanning the dark forest. "They'll be looking for us. We need to get back to the barn and regroup."

The group nodded and set off into the woods, their movements swift and silent. Erin lingered at the back of the group, her glowing eyes darting nervously between the trees. Logan fell into step beside her, his voice soft.

"You okay?" he asked.

Erin hesitated, then nodded. "I'm fine. I just... worried. The energy in the facility felt different this time. Stronger. Like the Rift is growing."

Logan's brow furrowed, but he kept his tone reassuring. "We'll figure it out. We always do."

Erin managed a small smile, her tension easing slightly. "Thanks, Logan."

When they reached the barn, the first hints of dawn were creeping over the horizon. The group collapsed onto their makeshift seats, exhaustion settling in as the adrenaline began to wear off.

"Alright, Jamari," Alex said, leaning forward. "Let's see what we're dealing with."

Jamari plugged the floppy disk into the adapter on his PDA, filling the screen with rows of encrypted files. "Give me a sec," he muttered, his fingers flying over the keyboard. After a few tense moments, a document opened, its header bold and ominous: **PROJECT NEXUS: RIFT CORE STABILIZATION AND CONTROL.**

"Control?" Sarah said, her voice sharp. "They're trying to control the Rift?"

"More than that," Jamari replied, scrolling through the file. "They've built something—a device called the Nexus Core. It's designed to stabilize the Rift and amplify its energy output. If they activate this thing, the Rift won't just stay open. It'll expand."

"Expand?" Max echoed, his eyes widening. "How much?"

Jamari hesitated, then pointed to a line in the document. "Enough to consume everything within a hundred-mile radius. And that's just the beginning."

The barn fell silent as the weight of Jamari's words sank in. Alex broke the silence, his voice firm. "Then we stop it. Whatever this Nexus Core is, we destroy it."

"It's not going to be that simple," Elias said, stepping out of the shadows. He had been listening quietly, his expression grim. "If the Core is active, it'll be heavily guarded. And if it's connected to the Rift, taking it out might have consequences we can't predict."

"Do we have a choice?" Sarah asked, her voice rising. "If we don't stop it, Helix Labs will turn this whole town into ground zero."

Elias nodded reluctantly. "You're right. But we need a plan—a real one. This isn't just sneaking into a lab. This is war."

Alex looked around at the group, their faces mixed with fear and determination. "Then we plan. We figure out how to get to the Core and take it out without losing anyone. Jamari, start decoding the rest of those files. Sarah, Logan, and I will work on recon. Max, you and Elias figure out what we need to fight back."

Erin spoke up, her voice quiet but firm. "And me? What do I do?"

Alex met her gaze, his expression softening. "You rest. You've done more than enough for now. When the time comes, we'll need you at full strength."

Erin nodded, though the faint flicker of unease in her glowing eyes remained. The sun rose as the group broke into their tasks, bathing the barn in light. They knew the battle ahead would test them in ways they couldn't yet imagine, but for now, they had hope—and each other.

Erin sat on a stack of hay bales in the corner of the barn, absent-mindedly tracing patterns in the dust on her knees. The others worked around her, their voices blending into a hum of strategizing and preparation. Logan appeared beside her, holding out a steaming cup of instant cocoa.

"Thought you could use this," he said, his grin crooked but warm.

Erin blinked in surprise and took the cup with a soft, "Thank you." She sipped it cautiously, the warmth spreading through her chilled hands.

"You've been quiet," Logan said, sitting down on the bale beside her. "Are you sure you're okay?"

"I keep thinking about the Rift," Erin admitted, her glowing eyes dim as they stared past him. "If it expands... if it becomes too strong, I might be unable to stop it."

Logan hesitated, then said, "You don't have to do it alone. Whatever happens, we're in this together."

Her gaze softened, meeting his. "You believe that, don't you?"

He shrugged, his grin widening. "It's kind of our thing."

Before Erin could respond, Alex's voice cut through the barn. "Everyone over here! We've got something."

The group gathered around Jamari, who had pulled another set of files on his PDA. The screen displayed a schematic labeled **Nexus Core Operational Protocol.**

"This file," Jamari began, pointing to the data, "explains how the Nexus Core connects to the Rift. It's designed to stabilize the energy fluctuations but also amplify them, which is why the Rift is expanding."

"So if we remove the Core, we destabilize the Rift," Alex concluded. "Does that mean it'll collapse?"

"Not exactly," Jamari said, frowning. "If we're not careful, taking out the Core could cause the Rift to spiral out of control. But if we can time it right—say, when the Rift is at its weakest point—we might be able to sever the connection completely."

"And when is it at its weakest?" Sarah asked.

Jamari hesitated, scrolling through the data. "Midnight. The Rift's energy levels dip at midnight every night, probably because of some temporal synchronization with Phyrexia."

"So we've got a time window," Alex said. "Midnight. One shot."

"What about Henshaw?" Max interjected. "He's not just going to let us waltz in and blow up his precious toy."

Elias stepped forward, arms crossed. "We'll have to split up. One team takes out the Core, and the other runs interference."

"I'll go with the Core team," Erin said immediately, her voice firm.

Alex shook his head. "Not a chance. It's too dangerous."

"I'm the only one who can resist the Rift's pull," Erin countered. "If the Core amplifies its energy while we're trying to destroy it, you'll need me to keep it in check."

Alex hesitated, clearly torn, but finally nodded. "Alright. You're in."

The group worked late into the night, refining their plan and preparing their gear. The barn was filled with tense anticipation by the time they were finished.

"Get some rest," Alex said as the group dispersed. "Tomorrow, we end this."

As Erin settled into her corner of the barn, she caught Logan's eye across the room. He gave her a reassuring nod, and for the first time since they'd left Helix Labs, she felt a glimmer of hope.

The following day, the barn was alive with activity as the group prepared for what lay ahead. Alex stood near the map they had pinned to the wall, reviewing their route to the Helix Labs facility one final time. His sharp eyes scanned every detail, searching for any potential weak spots in their plan.

Max paced in the background, his usual humor muted. "So we're doing this, huh? Storming the gates of evil and all that."

"Pretty much," Logan replied, tightening the straps on his pack. "You nervous?"

"Only as much as I should be," Max said with a faint grin. "You?"

"Same," Logan admitted. His gaze drifted to Erin sitting by the window, her glowing eyes fixed on the horizon. "But I think we're ready."

Sarah approached the table, her expression resolute. "I rechecked the escape routes. They're clear, but we must move fast once the Core is down. The place will go on full lockdown."

"Good," Alex said, nodding. "Jamari, what's the status of the files?"

Jamari, hunched over his PDA, looked up with a faint smirk. "Everything's decrypted. I've mapped out the Core's exact location. It's deep in the central lab, but the blueprints show a service elevator that should get us close. The tricky part will be bypassing the security grid."

Elias, leaning against a support beam, crossed his arms. "I've got some old tricks that might help with that. Let's hope Helix Labs hasn't upgraded since I last dealt with them."

Erin stood and walked over to the group, her movements steady despite the tension in her expression. "What happens if we can't stop it?" she asked quietly.

Alex met her gaze, his voice steady. "We don't let that happen."

For a moment, the barn was silent. Then Logan stepped forward, placing a reassuring hand on Erin's shoulder. "We've got this," he said. "Together."

Erin nodded, her glowing eyes brightening slightly. "Together."

As the sun rose higher in the sky, the group finished their preparations. They packed their backpacks, checked their weapons, and reviewed every detail of their plan until it became second nature.

Alex stood at the center of the barn, his voice cutting through the quiet. "This is it. We know the risks, but we also know what's at stake. Helix Labs doesn't care about the damage they're causing. We do. And we're the only ones who can stop them."

The group nodded, their resolve solidifying. Max clapped his hands together, breaking the tension. "Alright, let's go save the world. Again."

With that, they filed out of the barn, the weight of their mission pressing heavily on their shoulders. The path ahead was uncertain, but one thing was clear: they were ready to face whatever came their way.

Chapter 13: The Road to Helix Labs

The van rumbled over uneven roads as the group approached Helix Labs. The tension inside was palpable, the weight of their mission pressing down on them. Outside, the trees blurred into a sea of green, their dense canopy shielding the van from the rising sun.

Max sat in the back, trying to lighten the mood with his usual humor. "Alright, so what's the plan if we run into, I don't know, a hundred agents? We play dead, right? I've been practicing." He slumped dramatically, earning a weak chuckle from Sarah.

"We stick to the plan," Alex said firmly from the passenger seat. His eyes were fixed on the road ahead, his jaw set. "No improvising unless it's necessary."

"But it's us," Max countered, sitting upright. "When do we ever not improvise?"

"Let's hope today's the exception," Logan muttered, his hands steady on the wheel.

Erin sat quietly beside Max, clutching her stuffed alien. The glowing in her eyes was faint, almost subdued as if she were conserving every ounce of her strength. Logan glanced at her through the rearview mirror. "Are you good?" he asked.

She nodded. "Just thinking. The Rift's energy... it's stronger today. I can feel it."

Jamari, seated in the middle with his PDA balanced on his lap, spoke up. "That makes sense. The files said the Nexus Core is designed to amplify the Rift's power. The closer we get, the more you'll feel it."

"Great," Max said, leaning back. "Because everything about this trip needed to be more unsettling."

They parked the van in a secluded grove a mile from the facility. The group piled out, their boots crunching against the forest floor as they gathered their gear. Alex unfolded a map, spreading it over the van's hood.

"We're here," he said, pointing to a marked spot. "The facility's main entrance is heavily guarded, so we use the maintenance tunnel. Jamari, you lead us to the service elevator. Once we're in, we move fast."

Elias leaned over the map, his sharp eyes scanning the route. "We'll need a distraction to keep their eyes off the tunnel."

Sarah nodded, adjusting the straps on her backpack. "Leave that to me and Max. We can create enough noise to draw them away."

"You sure about that?" Logan asked, his brow furrowed.

Sarah smirked. "Don't worry. We'll be fine."

Alex clapped his hands together. "Alright, everyone knows their roles. Let's move."

The trek through the forest was silent but tense. The group's movements were careful and deliberate, their senses on high alert. Erin lingered near the back with Logan, her steps lighter than usual.

"You're quiet," Logan said softly, breaking the silence.

"Just focusing," Erin replied. "The Rift's pull is stronger than I expected. It's... distracting."

Logan reached out, giving her shoulder a reassuring squeeze. "You've got this. And we've got you."

She offered a faint smile, her glowing eyes meeting his momentarily. "Thanks, Logan."

They reached the maintenance tunnel without incident, the entrance obscured by thick underbrush. Alex and Logan quickly cleared the way, revealing a rusted metal hatch. Elias inspected the lock, pulling a small toolkit from his bag.

"This shouldn't take long," he muttered, his hands deftly working the mechanisms.

"Better not," Max whispered, his gaze darting around the forest. "Feels like we're being watched."

The lock clicked open, and Elias stepped back. "We're in."

The group descended into the tunnel, the air growing cooler and damp as they moved deeper underground. Jamari led the way, his PDA illuminating the path with a faint blue glow. Their footsteps echoed softly, a constant reminder of how vulnerable they were.

"We're close," Jamari said, his voice hushed. "The service elevator should be just ahead."

They reached a junction where the tunnel opened into a small maintenance hub. The elevator doors loomed before them, their metallic surface reflecting the dim light. Jamari stepped forward, connecting his PDA to the control panel.

"Give me a minute," he said, his fingers flying over the screen.

Erin's glowing eyes flickered as the group waited, her body tensing. "Something's wrong," she said, her voice tight.

Before anyone could respond, the faint sound of voices echoed from the tunnel behind them. Alex spun around, his grip tightening on his crowbar.

"Agents," he said. "We need to move. Now."

Jamari worked faster, sweat beading on his forehead. "Almost there," he muttered.

The voices grew louder, accompanied by the unmistakable sound of footsteps. Logan and Max moved to the rear, their weapons ready, and Alex motioned for the others to stay close to the elevator.

With a final beep, the elevator doors slid open. "Got it!" Jamari exclaimed.

"Go!" Alex shouted, ushering the group inside. As the doors began to close, the first agents appeared at the end of the tunnel, their shouts echoing through the chamber.

The elevator ascended, and the hum of its machinery was a welcome sound as the tension began to ease. But Alex's expression remained grim. "They know we're here," he said. "From this point on, we're on borrowed time."

The group exchanged determined glances as the elevator slowed to a stop. The doors slid open, revealing the stark, sterile halls of Helix Labs. The air was thick with the hum of machinery and the faint pulse of the Rift's energy.

"All right," Alex said, stepping out. "Let's finish this."

The group emerged cautiously from the elevator, their senses on high alert. The sterile white walls of Helix Labs seemed to close around them, the hum of machinery and the faint pulse of Rift energy ever-present.

"All right," Alex said hushedly, glancing at Jamari. "Which way?"

Jamari checked his PDA, his fingers deftly navigating the facility's layout. "Left, then down the hall. The Core is in the central lab, two floors up. But we'll need to bypass a security checkpoint to get there."

Elias stepped forward, his expression calm but focused. "Let me handle the checkpoint. If they haven't upgraded their systems, I should be able to disable the alarms."

"And if they have?" Max asked, gripping his makeshift weapon tighter.

Elias smirked faintly. "Then we improvise."

The group moved as one; their footsteps muffled against the pristine floor. Erin lingered near the middle of the pack, her glowing eyes darting nervously between the walls. The Rift's pull was stronger here, a constant hum in the back of her mind.

Logan fell into step beside her. "You holding up?" he asked quietly.

She nodded, though her hands trembled slightly. "It's just... loud. The Rift. It feels alive here."

"Stay close," Logan said, his tone reassuring. "We've got this."

They reached the first security checkpoint without incident. A large metal door blocked their path, a glowing keypad and security camera mounted beside it. Elias crouched by the panel, pulling a small device from his bag.

"Give me a minute," he muttered, connecting the device to the keypad. The screen flickered as he worked, lines of code scrolling rapidly.

"How much longer?" Sarah whispered, glancing nervously back down the hall.

"Almost there," Elias replied.

Suddenly, Erin's head snapped up, her eyes glowing brighter. "They're coming," she said urgently. "I can feel them."

"We're out of time," Alex said, gripping his crowbar. "Elias, can you speed it up?"

"Working on it," Elias replied, his voice tense. The door let out a soft hiss as it slid open. "Go!"

The group hurried through the door, Elias sealing it behind them. They paused briefly to catch their breath, their eyes scanning the dimly lit corridor ahead.

"We're getting closer," Jamari said, his PDA pinging softly. "The Core should be just above us."

"Then let's move," Alex said.

As they ascended a narrow stairwell, the air grew heavier, the hum of the Rift's energy intensifying with each step. When they reached the top, the hallway ahead was lined with glass panels, revealing glimpses of the lab beyond. Inside, scientists and agents moved with purpose; their attention focused on the pulsating energy emanating from a massive structure in the center of the room.

"The Nexus Core," Jamari whispered, his voice tinged with awe and dread.

The Core was a towering, mechanical construct, its surface pulsing with shifting lights and glowing energy lines. A swirling vortex of Rift energy crackled and writhed at its heart, casting eerie shadows across the room.

"How do we take it out?" Sarah asked, her voice barely audible.

Jamari glanced at his PDA. "Power conduits are running to the Core from three separate terminals. If we disable those, the Core should destabilize."

"And how long do we have before it blows?" Logan asked.

"Not long," Jamari admitted. "Once we start, we'll need to move fast."

Alex nodded, his expression grim. "Alright. Jamari, Erin, and I will handle the terminals. Logan, Sarah, Max, and Elias, you cover us. If anyone comes through that door, stop them."

The group exchanged determined glances. Alex took a deep breath, his voice steady. "This is it. Let's finish this."

As the group approached the Core, the atmosphere in the room shifted. The pulsing hum of the Nexus Core grew louder, the vibrations coursing through the floor and into their bones. The air felt electric, charged with the unstable energy of the Rift.

Alex turned to Jamari and Erin. "You two take the first terminal. I'll cover you while you disable it."

Logan, Max, Sarah, and Elias moved to position themselves near the entrance, weapons ready. The distant echo of footsteps and muffled voices grew louder, signaling the arrival of Helix Labs agents.

"We've got company," Elias said, gripping his weapon tightly. "Be ready."

Jamari worked quickly, his hands flying over the terminal's interface as he bypassed its security. Erin stood beside him, her glowing eyes fixed on the swirling vortex of the Nexus Core. She could feel its pull more strongly than ever, the Rift's chaotic energy calling to her almost irresistibly.

"I've got one down," Jamari announced, stepping back as the first power conduit shut down. A section of the Core dimmed slightly, but the rest continued to pulse and hum.

"Good," Alex said. "Move to the next one. I'll cover you."

Erin nodded, leading Jamari to the second terminal. But before they could begin, a loud crash echoed through the room as the agents breached the entrance.

"Here they come!" Sarah shouted, raising her weapon.

The team near the door sprang into action, their makeshift weapons clashing with the agents' high-tech gear. Logan swung his crowbar precisely, disarming one agent before ducking behind cover. Max used a length of pipe to deflect another agent's baton, his quick reflexes keeping him one step ahead.

"Focus on the terminals!" Alex yelled, fending off an agent who had broken through the defense.

Jamari's fingers moved faster, sweat dripping down his temple as he worked to turn off the second conduit. Erin stood guard, her hands glowing with energy as she prepared to unleash her powers if necessary. The Rift's pull was overwhelming now, but she gritted her teeth, determined to see this through.

"Second conduit down!" Jamari called, stepping back. Another section of the Core dimmed, its lights flickering erratically.

The agents seemed to grow more desperate, their movements frantic as they pushed harder against the group's defenses. Sarah swung her weapon with calculated force, her eyes blazing with determination. Elias fought with practiced efficiency, and his experience was evident in every move.

"One more," Alex said, gesturing for Jamari and Erin to move to the final terminal. "We're almost there."

As Jamari began working on the last terminal, Erin's eyes locked onto the Core. The swirling vortex seemed to respond to her presence, its energy reaching out like tendrils of light. She stepped closer, her glowing eyes intensifying.

"Erin?" Logan called, his voice tinged with worry. "What are you doing?"

"It's calling to me," she said softly. "I think I can... contain it."

"Not alone, you can't," Alex said firmly. "Stick to the plan."

Jamari's PDA beeped as the final conduit shut down. The Core shuddered, its lights flickering wildly as the vortex within began to destabilize.

"We did it!" Jamari exclaimed, stepping back. "The Core is shutting down!"

But the victory was short-lived. A deafening roar echoed through the room as creatures from the Rift began to emerge, their distorted forms twisting and writhing as they materialized. The Rift's energy surged, filling the air with an oppressive heat.

"Fall back!" Alex shouted, raising his crowbar. "Protect Jamari and Erin!"

The group formed a defensive circle, their weapons raised as the creatures advanced. Erin stepped forward, her hands glowing brighter than ever. She closed her eyes, focusing all her energy on the Rift.

"I can do this," she whispered, her voice steady despite the chaos around her.

As the creatures closed in, the group braced themselves for the battle, their determination unwavering. The fate of Shadowridge—and possibly the world—rested on their shoulders.

Chapter 14: Rift's Fury

The Nexus Core shuddered violently, its swirling vortex pulsating erratically as the creatures continued to emerge. Shadows twisted and writhed, transforming into grotesque, otherworldly forms that moved with unnatural speed and fluidity. The air crackled with energy, the hum of the Rift growing louder with each passing second.

"Hold the line!" Alex shouted, positioning himself between the group and the advancing creatures. His crowbar swung in a wide arc, connecting with a creature's jagged limb and sending it stumbling back.

Max let out a yelp as a second creature lunged at him. "This was not part of the plan!" he exclaimed, swinging his pipe wildly. Logan stepped in, his crowbar landing a solid blow that sent the creature crashing into the lab's metal walls.

"They just keep coming!" Sarah shouted, slamming her makeshift weapon into a creature attempting to climb onto a nearby console.

"Focus on protecting Erin!" Alex yelled. "She's the only one who can stop this!"

Erin stood near the Core, her glowing eyes locked on the vortex. The energy radiating from it seemed to resonate with her, and she took a deep breath, centering herself. Her hands began to glow brighter, pulsating with the same rhythm as the Rift.

"I need more time!" Erin called out, her voice steady but strained. "I'm almost ready!"

Jamari worked furiously at a nearby terminal, where his PDA was connected to the lab's systems. "I'm trying to redirect power away from the Core!" he shouted. "If I can cut the energy flow, it might slow the Rift down!"

"Make it fast!" Elias barked, slamming the butt of his weapon into a creature's head. "We're running out of room to fight!"

The creatures were relentless, their numbers seemingly endless. One broke through the defensive line, heading straight for Erin. Logan intercepted it, tackling the beast and driving it back with fierce blows.

"Stay away from her!" he growled, his voice filled with determination.

"Thanks," Erin said softly, her focus never wavering from the Core.

The room seemed to warp as the Rift's energy reached a fever pitch. Erin's glow intensified, spreading outward in waves that pushed the creatures back momentarily. She stepped closer to the Core, her hands raised as she channeled her energy into the vortex.

"I can see it," Erin murmured, her voice distant. "I can feel the Rift's connection. It's... alive."

"What does that mean?" Sarah asked, her voice sharp as she struck down another creature.

"It's fighting me," Erin replied, her brow furrowing. "But I can weaken it. Just a little more..."

The ground beneath them trembled as the Core began to destabilize further. Sparks flew from the power conduits, and the air grew heavy with heat and static. The creatures faltered momentarily, their forms flickering as if tethered to the Rift's instability.

"It's working!" Jamari exclaimed, glancing at his PDA. "The energy levels are dropping!"

"Keep going, Erin!" Alex encouraged, stepping in front of her to block another advancing creature.

With a final, piercing scream, Erin thrust her hands forward, a surge of blue light erupting from her body and colliding with the vortex. The Core buckled under the force, its structure cracking as the Rift's energy began to collapse inward.

"It's collapsing!" Jamari shouted. "Everyone, get back!"

Alex grabbed Erin, pulling her away from the Core as the group retreated toward the elevator. The creatures let out unearthly howls, their forms disintegrating one by one as the Rift's connection was severed. The Nexus Core imploded, sending a shockwave through the lab that knocked the group off their feet.

When the dust settled, the room was eerily quiet. The Rift's hum was gone, replaced by the faint crackle of dying sparks. The Core was nothing more than a smoldering heap of metal and wires.

Erin lay on the ground, her breathing shallow but steady. Logan knelt beside her, his expression filled with concern. "Erin? Are you okay?"

She opened her eyes slowly, the glow dim but present. "I'm... okay," she whispered. "It's over."

Alex stood, surveying the wreckage. "We did it," he said, his voice heavy with relief. "The Rift is closed."

But as the group began to regroup, Elias's sharp voice cut through the quiet. "We need to move. Henshaw won't let this go unanswered. We've bought ourselves some time, but not much."

The group nodded, their exhaustion giving way to determination. The battle was over, but the war against Helix Labs was far from finished.

As the group stumbled back toward the elevator, the weight of their victory began to sink in. The once-imposing Core was now a smoking ruin, its connection to the Rift severed. But the reality of what they had just faced left them shaken.

"Did anyone see how many of those things came through?" Max asked, his voice tight with lingering adrenaline. "It felt like an army."

Sarah wiped the sweat from her brow, her weapon still clutched tightly in her hand. "If Erin hadn't stopped it..." She trailed off, shaking her head. "We wouldn't have made it."

Erin, still leaning heavily on Logan, managed a weak smile. "We made it because we're a team. And because Logan kept the creatures off me long enough to finish the job."

Logan grinned down at her. "Just doing my part. You're the real MVP here, Erin."

Jamari, still glued to his PDA, looked up with a worried expression. "Not to ruin the moment, but we've got another problem. The explosion's going to alert every agent in this place. If Henshaw's not already on his way, he will be soon."

"He's right," Elias said, his tone grim. "We need to get out of here. Fast."

Alex nodded, gripping his crowbar tightly. "Alright. Logan, help Erin. Jamari, keep tracking their movements. We'll take the tunnels back out, but we stick together. No one gets left behind."

The group moved quickly, retracing their steps through the labyrinth of Helix Labs. The air was thick with smoke and the acrid smell of burning machinery, making every breath a struggle. Erin's glow had dimmed significantly, and her energy drained, but she pressed on with Logan's steady support.

The sound of distant voices and pounding footsteps echoed through the halls, growing louder with each passing moment. Alex gestured for the group to duck into a side corridor, holding a hand for silence.

"Agents," he whispered, peeking around the corner. A squad of heavily armed men marched past, their weapons raised and their eyes scanning for intruders. The group held their breath, waiting until the footsteps faded.

"That was too close," Sarah muttered as they resumed their escape.

The tunnel entrance finally came into view, but it was blocked by a steel grate that hadn't been there before. Jamari cursed under his breath as he knelt to inspect it. "They must've locked it down after we came in. Give me a minute."

"We don't have a minute," Elias said, eyes scanning the corridor behind them.

Erin stepped forward, placing a hand on the grate. Her glow flickered, then brightened as she focused her remaining energy. The metal groaned, bending and twisting until a narrow opening appeared.

"That's all I can do," she said, swaying slightly.

"It's enough," Alex said, helping her through the gap. The others followed, squeezing through the twisted metal and into the relative safety of the tunnel.

The group didn't stop moving until they emerged into the cool night air, their lungs filling with much-needed fresh oxygen. The forest was quiet, starkly contrasting the chaos they had left behind.

Alex turned to the group, his expression a mix of relief and determination. "We did it. We stopped the Core. But this isn't over. Helix Labs won't stop, and neither will we."

Elias nodded, his face set in a grim line. "We've bought ourselves some time, but Henshaw won't let this go. We need to regroup and figure out our next move."

Erin looked at each of them, her voice quiet but resolute. "Whatever comes next, we'll face it together. We've already proven we can."

The group exchanged weary smiles, their bond more potent than ever despite their challenges. As they returned to Shadowridge, the first hints of dawn began to break over the horizon, painting the sky in shades of pink and gold. It was a new day—and their fight was far from over.

Chapter 15: Facing the Aftermath

The morning light cast long shadows across the barn as the group trudged inside, their exhaustion palpable. The quiet hum of early birdsong contrasted with the chaos they had left behind at Helix Labs. Each member carried the weight of their mission—and the knowledge that their victory was only a reprieve.

With a dull thud, Alex dropped his crowbar onto the makeshift table and turned to the others. "Alright, first things first. Is anyone hurt?"

Logan glanced at Erin, who was leaning heavily against him. "She's wiped out, but I think she'll be okay."

"I'm fine," Erin said softly, though her glowing eyes were faint, indicating her depleted energy. "Just need to rest."

"You've earned it," Sarah said, reassuringly smiling as she guided Erin to a pile of blankets in the corner. "Take all the time you need."

Max plopped down on a crate, running a hand through his hair. "I'd say we all need a break. But something tells me Henshaw's not going to give us one."

Elias, who had been standing near the barn door, nodded grimly. "You're right. He'll come after us harder than ever now. Taking out the Core was a major blow to Helix Labs, but it won't stop them. If anything, it'll make them more dangerous."

Jamari pulled out his PDA, scanning through the recovered data. "We need to figure out what's next. The files we pulled before the Core went down—there has to be something in here we can use."

"Let's start with what we know," Alex said, his tone steady despite his fatigue. "We stopped the Rift for now, but that doesn't mean it's gone for good. And Helix Labs still has other facilities. If they regroup, they could try this again."

"Or worse," Sarah added. "What if they've already started?"

The barn fell silent, the weight of her words settling over them like a heavy fog. Erin stirred, her voice quiet but firm. "We'll stop them," she said. "Whatever it takes."

As the group began to sift through the data, the tension in the barn eased slightly, replaced by a sense of focused determination. Jamari's fingers flew over his PDA as he pieced together fragments of encrypted files. Logan and Max worked to reinforce the barn's defenses while Sarah brewed a pot of coffee, the rich aroma filling the air.

Elias stood by the window, his sharp eyes scanning the horizon. "We'll need allies if we're going to keep this up," he said. "People we can trust."

Alex looked up from the table, his expression thoughtful. "You know anyone who fits that description?"

"Maybe," Elias replied. "But reaching out to them is a risk. If Helix Labs gets wind of it, it could endanger them."

"We're already in danger," Logan said, rejoining the group. "If there are people who can help, we need to find them. We can't do this alone."

Alex nodded. "Alright. Elias, see what you can do. We will keep working on the files and determine our next move."

As the day wore on, the group fell into a rhythm, their exhaustion tempered by their resolve. Erin slept soundly in the corner, breathing steady as she regained strength. Jamari finally released a triumphant "Got it!" as he cracked another layer of encryption, his screen filling with schematics and reports.

"What is it?" Alex asked, leaning over his shoulder.

Jamari pointed to a document labeled **Project Genesis." "It's another experiment. Bigger than the Nexus Core. And it's already in motion."

The group gathered around, their expressions grim as they read through the details. The document described a plan to open multiple Rifts simultaneously, using a network of smaller cores spread across the country.

"They're trying to create a stable gateway," Jamari explained. "Something they can control. If they succeed..."

"It'll make the Nexus Core look like a test run," Elias finished, his voice heavy.

Alex clenched his fists, his jaw tightening. "Then we stop it. We find out where these cores are and shut them down before they can activate."

Sarah looked at the group, her gaze steady. "We've faced worse and come out stronger. We can do this."

Erin stirred, sitting up slowly. Her glowing eyes were brighter now, and her expression showed a renewed sense of purpose. "We don't have a choice," she said. "If they open those Rifts, it won't just be Shadowridge. It'll be everywhere."

The group exchanged determined glances, their bond unshaken despite the challenges ahead. They had stopped the Nexus Core, but their fight against Helix Labs was far from over. And this time, the stakes were higher than ever.

As the gravity of Project Genesis settled over the group, the barn grew quiet once more. Each member wrestled with the implications of Helix Labs' ambitions, their resolve hardening with every passing moment.

Sarah broke the silence, her voice cutting through the tension. "So, where do we start? How do we even find these cores?"

Jamari tapped his PDA, bringing up a map with several blinking points. "The files include a list of potential sites. It's incomplete, but it gives us somewhere to begin. Most of them are remote, places no one would think to look."

Alex studied the map, finger-tracing a route from Shadowridge to the nearest marked location. "This one's only a couple of hours away. We'll hit it first. If it's active, we shut it down. If not, we move to the next."

"Sounds straightforward," Logan said, folding his arms. "But what happens if we run into another Rift or worse, Henshaw?"

"We'll deal with it," Alex said firmly. "The same way we always do—together."

Max, who had been uncharacteristically quiet, finally spoke up. "Let's just hope we're not walking into a trap. Helix Labs isn't stupid. They'll be expecting us."

Elias nodded in agreement. "Max is right. We need to be ready for anything. Before we leave, I'll see what I can scrounge up regarding supplies and intel."

Alex turned to Jamari. "Keep digging through those files. If there's anything we can use—blueprints, schedules, anything—it could make all the difference."

Jamari gave a quick nod. "You got it."

Later that evening, as the sun dipped below the horizon, casting the barn in a warm amber glow, Erin sat outside on an old wooden bench. The cool breeze carried the scent of pine and earth, a small comfort after the chaos of the past days.

Logan stepped out, his boots crunching softly against the gravel. He approached her with a hesitant smile, holding two mugs of steaming coffee. "Figured you could use this," he said, handing her one.

"Thanks," Erin said, cradling the mug in her hands. The warmth seeped into her fingers, chasing away the chill.

They sat in companionable silence for a while, the distant sounds of the others working inside drifting through the open barn doors. Finally, Logan spoke. "You were amazing back there. With the Core, I mean. I don't think we'd have made it without you."

Erin glanced at him, her glowing eyes soft in the fading light. "It wasn't just me. We all played a part."

"Yeah," Logan said, his grin widening. "But you were the MVP."

Erin smiled faintly, looking down at her mug. "I just hope I can keep doing what's needed. The Rift... it feels like it's a part of me. Like I can't escape it."

"You don't have to," Logan said gently. "Whatever happens, you've got us. We've got your back."

Erin's smile grew a little more potent. "Thanks, Logan. That means a lot."

Inside the barn, the group continued to prepare for the journey ahead. Alex and Elias worked on reinforcing their equipment while Sarah pored over the map with Jamari, identifying the best routes and contingency plans.

Max paced near the doorway, his usual humor returning. "So, do we have a code name for this mission yet? 'Operation Shut Down the Apocalypse' has a nice ring."

Sarah rolled her eyes but couldn't suppress a small laugh. "How about 'Operation Don't Get Caught'?"

"Now that's just boring," Max replied, grinning.

Alex looked up from his work, his face grave but not unkind. "How about 'Operation Genesis'? That's what we're stopping, after all."

The group nodded in agreement, the name settling over them like a rallying cry. As the night deepened, their laughter and banter gave way to quiet determination. They knew the road ahead would be dangerous, but they were ready to face it—together.

As dawn broke over Shadowridge, the barn seemed to hum with quiet resolve. Each member of the group worked steadily, finalizing preparations for their next mission. The air was heavy with the unspoken acknowledgment that their fight was far from over and that Helix Labs was already planning its next move.

Logan and Erin sat on the old wooden bench outside the barn. The glow in Erin's eyes had returned, faint but steady, as she stared into the distance. Logan leaned back, watching her thoughtfully.

"You've been quiet," he said after a moment. "What's on your mind?"

Erin hesitated, then turned to face him. "I've been thinking about what happens next. About the Rift, and Helix Labs, and… us."

Logan raised an eyebrow, a teasing smile tugging at his lips. "Us?"

Her cheeks flushed faintly, the glow in her eyes flickering. "I mean all of us. The group. What we're up against."

"Right," Logan said, though his grin softened into something gentler. "Well, for what it's worth, I think we'll figure it out. Together."

Erin smiled, her gaze dropping to the ground. "You always know what to say."

"Part of my charm," Logan replied, nudging her lightly with his shoulder. "But seriously, Erin. You're not alone in this. We've got your back. And… I've got your back. Always."

Erin looked up at him, her expression shifting from uncertainty to something brighter, more hopeful. "Thanks, Logan. That means more than you know."

The world seemed to fall away for a moment, leaving only the two of them in the morning stillness. Logan reached for her hand, and she didn't pull away. The connection was simple but profound, a promise forged in the quiet chaos of their shared fight.

Inside the barn, Alex watched the exchange from the window, a small smile tugging at his lips. Sarah walked up beside him, following his gaze.

"Looks like they're finally figuring it out," Sarah said, her tone light.

"About time," Alex replied. "They've been dancing around it long enough."

Sarah chuckled, then sobered. "Think we're ready for what's next?"

"We have to be," Alex said, his expression growing serious. "Helix Labs isn't going to stop, and neither can we. This is just the beginning."

Sarah nodded, her resolve matching his. "Then let's make sure it counts."

As the group gathered around the map one last time, their mission clear, the barn seemed to pulse with energy—not just from the challenges ahead but also from the bond that had formed between them. They were more than a group of friends now; they were a family united by a common goal and an unshakable determination.

"Alright," Alex said, his voice steady. "We know what we're up against. Let's get moving."

The group exchanged determined glances, their resolve solid as they prepared to embark on the next leg of their journey.

In the distance, the faint hum of the Rift still lingered, a reminder of the battles yet to come. But for the first time in what felt like forever, they faced it with hope.